CALEB THE PREACHER

CALEB
THE PREACHER

by
L. D. Tetlow

Dales Large Print Books
Long Preston, North Yorkshire,
England.

British Library Cataloguing in Publication Data.

Tetlow, L. D.
  Caleb the preacher.

A catalogue record for this book is
available from the British Library

ISBN 1-85389-644-6 pbk

First published in Great Britain by Robert Hale Ltd., 1994

Copyright © 1994 by L. D. Tetlow

The right of L.D. Tetlow to be identified as author of
this work has been asserted by him in accordance with
the Copyright, Designs and Patents Act, 1988

Published in Large Print June, 1996 by arrangement with
Robert Hale Ltd.

Dales Large Print is an imprint of
Library Magna Books Ltd.
Printed and bound in Great Britain by
T.J. Press (Padstow) Ltd., Cornwall, PL28 8RW.

ONE

'Thou shalt not commit adultery!' the voice of the Reverend Caleb Black boomed out, as he looked accusingly at the congregation packed into the church in the small town of Reno.

His accusing gaze made many of the women avert their gaze to the floor and most of the men sit upright in self-righteous indignation. The fact that the Reverend Black, as well as being black by name was also black by race, while all but one small group of congregation were white, did not go down too well.

It had been many months since Reno had had a visiting preacher and most of the previous day had been taken up with three weddings and four baptisms, two of the baptisms the children of weddings conducted earlier.

'How many of you...'—his almost sneer-

7

ing gaze once more swept his captive audience —'can truly say that they have never broken this commandment?' His keen eyes did not miss the quick sideways glances between various men and women of different families and he smiled, making a mental note. 'I see that few of you can make such a claim. However, I am not here to sit in judgement on your past mis-deeds, there is still time to seek the forgiveness of the Lord. To those who have sinned, I say repent while you can, mend your ways and be true to God and His Commandments. To those of you who have not yet actually committed adultery, I say to you that even to look upon a man or woman with lust in your heart is as much an adulterous act as the very act itself...'

At this point there was a disturbance at the back of the church as three dirty, mean-looking men pushed the door open, their guns in their hands.

'Carry on preachin', Preacher!' barked one of the men. 'We're gonna do the collectin'!'

There were several stifled screams from

some of the women and children who were clamped close, but there was no panic. The three men slowly moved down the centre aisle, each passing a small sack along each row as he came to it.

'Just put all you've got into the sacks!' ordered the man again. 'That means everythin'; all the cash you've got, all your rings, watches an' even them fancy cufflinks I see some of you men are wearin'.'

'This is outrageous!' spluttered one old man, with a very military bearing. 'I'll see to it that you're...'

'You can see to what the hell you like!' laughed another outlaw. 'Just make sure you put everythin' you've got into the sack. You, Preacher, you were told to carry on preachin', so preach!'

The Reverend Caleb Black smiled slightly as he watched the three small sacks being filled. 'And the Lord said...'— he moved away from the altar and slowly made his way to the aisle, where he stood alongside the first rows of pews—'if thine right eye offend thee, pluck it out...'—his hands slipped casually into the pockets of his black, frock coat—'for it would be better that one of thy members should perish...'

Two of the outlaws were standing directly in front of the preacher and the other by the door. There was a slight movement from the preacher as his voice once again boomed out.

'And verily, I say unto you...'—he looked directly at the two men in front of him —'thine eye doth offend me greatly!'

There were two shots in quick succession and a third as the preacher moved to one side. Amid terrified screams and wails from the children, the three outlaws crashed to the wooden floor, one of their guns firing harmlessly into the floor. The Reverend Black was quickly astride one of the men, kicking his gun from his hand as he made a weak attempt to raise it.

'And I say unto you, if thine right hand offend thee, cut it off!'

By that time his words were drowned by the clatter of panic as everyone tried to squeeze through the narrow door at once. The preacher smiled, picked up the three sacks and waited until the congregation had fled into the street. Some of them, mainly the women, picked up or pushed their children and ran from the vicinity of the church while most of the men remained. They were joined by other townsfolk who had heard the shooting. Caleb Black checked on the three bodies and was quite satisfied that they were dead and then marched grandly from the church.

'I suggest that someone call the undertaker!' he commanded to nobody in particular.

'What the hell's been goin' on?' demanded a voice, with some authority.

'Ah, Sheriff!' greeted Caleb Black. 'There are three bodies inside the church; kindly have them removed at once, the House of God is not the place for them.'

Several people tried talking to the sheriff at once, and he had to silence them and looked demandingly at the preacher.

'Well?' he rasped. 'Maybe you'd better explain!'

'Quite simple,' the preacher smiled,

disarmingly. 'The three men now lying dead inside the church, tried to rob the entire congregation. Isn't that right?' He looked at two men who had been in church and they nodded dumbly. 'I really couldn't allow such a thing to happen in church,' continued the preacher, 'especially a church in which I was preaching.'

'You shot 'em?' asked the sheriff, incredulously.

'There was no other way,' replied the preacher, blandly. 'I doubt very much if they would have been amenable to reason, even from me, and I can be very persuasive when I need to be.'

'I don't believe this!' exclaimed the sheriff. 'This I've got to see!'

He marched into the church, closely followed by the Reverend Black and the elderly man with the military bearing. For a few moments the sheriff gazed down at the three bodies and grunted.

'A beautiful example of military thinking,' said the elderly man. 'The preacher lulled them into a false sense of security before doing what he had to. May I be the first to offer my congratulations, sir....' He extended his thin hand which the preacher took, smiling contentedly. 'Colonel George Baker, Fifth Cavalry, retired.'

'Thank you, Colonel,' replied the preacher. 'I too once served in the cavalry, the Third.'

'Third, eh?' said the colonel. 'Yes, I did hear the third had a black detachment...'

'I was commanding officer of that detachment,' said the preacher, with a wry smile. He could tell that it was taking all the colonel's grit to acknowledge a black man. 'Lieutenant Caleb Black.'

'Lieutenant, eh?' muttered the colonel. 'Well done.'

'If you two have quite finished talkin' about your army days,' interrupted the sheriff. 'I want to see you, Reverend, in my office. I'll talk to you later, Colonel.'

'What about my money, and my cuff-links?' demanded the colonel.

Caleb Black handed the three small sacks to the sheriff. 'He means what's in here,' he explained. 'Those men ordered everyone to put all their valuables and cash into these sacks. I think almost everyone had done so, perhaps there were a few at the front who had not.'

'You can collect it from my office, later,' said the sheriff. 'I've got to make an inventory of what's in them an' then folk can claim back what's theirs, providin' they can describe what they claim is theirs.'

'How can one describe money?' blustered the colonel. 'I put twelve dollars in there, as well as my cufflinks...I must insist...'

'You're not in the army now, Colonel!' reminded the sheriff. 'You ain't in no position to order anyone nor insist on nothin'; I'm the law round here an' if I say you've got to wait an' then describe your goods, then you've got to wait. Got that?'

'I'll have your badge for this, McCauley!' the colonel blustered again. 'I am a prominent member of the town council...'

'Then you ought to be setting an example,' smiled the preacher, deliberately putting his arm around the colonel's shoulder, just to feel him cringe at the touch of a black man. 'The sheriff is quite right, you must see that; he has to be certain that only those entitled to claim are allowed to do so.'

The colonel pulled away from the preacher and glowered at them both. 'Just remember that twelve dollars of the money belongs to me, no matter how much anyone else claims is theirs!'

'I'll remember, Colonel,' said the sheriff. 'Come on, Reverend, let's sort this out in my office.'

On the way to his office, the sheriff called at the undertaker's yard and told him to collect the bodies, assuring the worried little man that his expenses would be met out of town funds.

'Now then,' said Sheriff Matt McCauley as he offered the preacher a seat in front of his desk. 'Maybe you'd better explain again, precisely what happened. It would seem to me that you must have been the only person who saw everythin', since they were all lookin' at you.'

The preacher smiled indulgently and patiently explained in the minutest detail what had happened. When he had finished,

McCauley smiled and tipped out the contents of the sacks and studied each item closely.

'Not a bad haul,' he had to admit. 'Most the folks in the church were from outlyin' farms. All of 'em are always pleadin' poverty an' most the men spend every Saturday night tryin' to bum drinks off other folk.' He laughed coarsely. 'The women pretend they're pure an' loyal to their menfolk, but I'd say that none of 'em ain't averse to earnin' a little extra money on the side, 'specially when the boys from the big ranches hit town. I reckon all their men also know exactly what their virtuous wives are up to, but they don't bother, providin' it brings in extra money.'

'I had the feeling that might be the case,' smiled Caleb. 'I could see it from the looks on their faces.'

'And some fell upon stony ground!' quoted the sheriff.

'And there appears to be an awful lot of stony ground out there!' laughed Caleb. 'However, it is not about the morals of farmers that I am concerned at this moment. I would think I am correct in assuming that those three men have, if not in this State then in others, a reward out on them.'

The sheriff looked up sharply at the rather forbidding black man who, even when seated, seemed to tower above everything. Standing, the Reverend Caleb Black was something over six feet six inches and almost as broad, or so it seemed.

'I reckon there could be,' he smiled. 'What's it to you though, Reverend? I wouldn't've thought a man of the cloth would have been interested in such things.'

'God may provide a great many things,' laughed Caleb, 'but I have yet to be blessed by Him with not having to eat or pay my way as I travel. The garb of a preacher is not a passport to a life of ease and cheap living. On the contrary, it would appear that prices in the shops suddenly rise by at least half should I show an interest in purchasing anything. I must confess that the situation is probably not helped by the colour of my skin. Black preachers are not that rare, but a black preacher who is prepared to defend himself by the use of a gun is very rare indeed. Unfortunately, I am driven to these remote parts out of necessity. In my home State, I had built up quite a reputation and there were a great many gunfighters only too ready to test me.'

'Not just one gun,' said the sheriff. 'I see you carry two. You're the first man I ever met who could use two guns at once.'

'I am what they call ambidextrous,' smiled Caleb. 'I am equally at home with either hand, be it holding a gun or holding a pen.'

Matt McCauley smiled and went to a cabinet, where he looked through a pile of Wanted posters. He finally grunted and pulled three posters out of the pile.

'You're in luck, Reverend,' he said. 'Hank Gibson, two hundred dollars for armed robbery and assault...'

He handed the poster to the preacher. 'James Ellison, two hundred for bank robbery an' Mick Fingerman, known as

Fingers, eight hundred for murder, bank robbery and assault. One thousand two hundred dollars; not a bad day's work. It oughta pay your expenses for a while.'

'It will certainly come in useful,' agreed Caleb. He had been looking with interest at the pile of posters in the cabinet. 'I wonder, Sheriff,' he said, 'would it be asking too much if I were to look through those posters? I like to know who I am likely to meet wherever I am, especially outlaws.'

McCauley smiled and waved his hand in the direction of the cabinet. 'Be my guest,' he invited, 'but I don't reckon it's just 'cos you want to know who you're liable to meet, I get me this feelin' this ain't the first time you've done somethin' like this.'

Caleb laughed a little and nodded. 'I must confess that of late, recovering reward money has made up the greatest part of my income.'

'Bounty huntin', you mean!' grinned McCauley.

'Such an ugly way of putting it,' sighed

19

the preacher. 'I look upon myself as a sort of sheriff or marshal. I am simply an instrument by which evil is brought to justice.'

'Like I said, a bounty hunter!' grinned the sheriff.

'I shall not trade words with you, Sheriff,' said Caleb. 'What I choose to call myself will make no difference. That colonel, Baker I believe he called himself, do you really believe that he was a colonel in the Fifth Cavalry?'

'Ain't got no cause not to believe him,' replied McCauley. 'I know there was a Colonel Baker in the Fifth, that's good enough for me.'

'But not for me,' smiled the preacher. 'I was a lieutenant in the Third, but I was sent on loan to the Fifth once. I met a Colonel Baker then, but it was certainly not the man who lives in your town who calls himself by that name or rank.'

'Are you sayin' he ain't Colonel Baker?'

'His name may well be George Baker,' said Caleb. 'All that I am saying is, unless there were two Colonels George Baker in the Fifth Cavalry, he is not of the rank he claims.'

McCauley shrugged. 'Don't see as it matters what he was or is; he's lived in Reno for the past three years an' never been no trouble. He's as good an' honest a citizen as you're ever likely to meet anywhere. He can call himself President of the United States for all I care.'

'It is more than likely that he calls himself colonel simply because he wants to impress,' agreed Caleb. 'However, I cannot help but think that had he been the real Colonel George Baker, he would have retired somewhere more appropriate than a nowhere town in the middle of a dusty plain, called Reno.'

'I reckon he's got his reasons,' shrugged McCauley. 'Whatever they are, they ain't no concern of mine.'

'You could be right,' agreed Caleb.

'Anyhow,' said the sheriff, 'you claim to be a preacher. How the hell do I know that? How the hell does anyone here know that? You performed three weddings yesterday. How can we be sure they're legal?'

Caleb smiled and produced a black wallet, from which he took a paper and handed to the sheriff. 'That says who I am and who ordained me,' he said. 'If you require further proof, I suggest you send a wire to the address at the bottom.'

'I'll take your word for it,' grinned McCauley. 'It won't matter none to any of them out there, even those you married. As far as they'll be concerned, it's all legal 'cos that's how they want it. I ain't in the business of shatterin' dreams, not even Colonel George Baker's.'

'I agree,' smiled Caleb. 'Even so, I can't help but wonder about our Colonel.'

'Then ask him!' suggested the sheriff.

'I might just do that!' grinned the preacher. 'Now, about my money, how long will it take?'

'No more'n two days,' replied the sheriff. 'In the meantime I'd appreciate it if you were to keep your activities to preachin' an' preacher's business. We ain't had a preacher in Reno for a long time, so there's sure to be some work for you, but I don't reckon it'd be a good idea to hang about too long, most the folks in these parts ain't too fond of blacks, not even black preachers.'

'I had that feeling,' said Caleb. 'Very well, as soon as you have the money, I shall move on; I have no desire to stay anywhere I am not wanted.'

'OK, that's fine by me,' said McCauley. 'I'm goin' to talk to some of the others now; you can look through the posters if you want. There's more'n one copy of most of 'em, help yourself to any you like.'

'I thank you, Sheriff,' said Caleb. 'I will not be too long.'

'You know,' said McCauley, 'for a black, you sure speak good English, proper I mean, very precise and correct.'

'Hardly that, Sheriff,' laughed Caleb, 'but I do have the advantage of a good education, which seems denied most of my brothers. I am not of slave stock: my father was a seaman out of Boston and my mother a freewoman from that same town. They made sure that I had the best education they could afford. Unfortunately I do not think they would approve of my present lifestyle.'

'Don't they know?'

'Oh, they knew I had chosen to be a preacher, but they knew nothing of my abilities or liking for guns. Fortunately, or unfortunately as you may see it, they are both now dead. They died of some disease my father caught on his voyages.'

'Sorry to hear that,' said McCauley. 'Now, I've got to talk to them farmers before they head back.'

'I doubt they will leave before they have reclaimed their property,' smiled Caleb.

'Maybe not,' agreed McCauley, 'but I've still got to hear their side of what happened.'

The property on the desk was scooped into a drawer which was locked, the sheriff making some laughing comment about not trusting even preachers. Caleb Black ignored the comment and slowly thumbed his way through the Wanted posters, taking a copy of each one.

As he left the sheriff's office, some twenty minutes later, Caleb was met by a black man, almost as big as himself. He had seen this man and his family in the church earlier, the only black people in town, or so it seemed.

The man looked quite smart but very uncomfortable dressed in what was plainly his Sunday best. He removed his hat in deference and coughed nervously.

'Ah hope you don't mind, Reveren',' he drawled, 'but me an' mah good lady, Pearl, was wonderin' if you would do us the honour of eatin' with us this evenin'. It ain't often we have a black brother in town, 'specially a preacher. We ain't got no fancy food an' the like, but we'd be mighty honoured to share what we do have.'

'Why certainly, brother!' beamed Caleb. 'I'd be more than honoured to share your table.'

'You would?' The man seemed very surprised.

'Sure thing, why not?' laughed Caleb.

'Well, Reveren',' gasped the man, 'Pearl said as how you wouldn't want to be seen with poor folk like us; she said as how you was probably used to better food, good beds an' good livin'. We cain't offer none of those things, but...'

'I haven't tasted good, black cookin' since I was in Boston,' laughed Caleb. 'Do you want me to come along now?'

'Yes, sir!' beamed a delighted black face. 'Aaron's the name, Aaron Williams, my wife is Pearl an' my...'

'Save the introductions for when I meet them,' said Caleb. 'Now, Aaron, lead on, I must confess to being hungry.'

'Yes, sir, Reveren', sir!' Aaron Williams puffed out his chest, proudly, and escorted his important guest along the street. The whole town stopped and stared, not at Aaron Williams, but at the preacher who had gunned down three outlaws in church.

Aaron lived in a rather tumbledown shack on the edge of town, not too far from the town rubbish dump, which imparted a not too pleasant aroma when the wind was in a certain direction, as it was at that moment. Caleb wrinkled his nose, wondered if he had made a wise

26

decision or not, but followed Aaron into the shack.

He was more than surprised at the interior of the shack. From the outside it appeared tumbledown, but inside, every effort had obviously been made to make a comfortable, clean home. The cooking from the spotlessly clean kitchen made Caleb feel very hungry. The last time he had smelled anything like it, it had been cooked by his mother.

'Chicken!' he drooled. 'Spicy chicken! I haven't tasted that since...oh, it's been a long time.'

'Best cook in the whole of the United States!' beamed Aaron. 'See Pearl, Ah told you he'd come. Reveren', Ah want you to meet the best cook, the best mother an' the best wife any man could ever have, my wife Pearl!' Aaron was clearly very fond of his wife. 'Pearl, the Reveren' Black. Ah don't know your given name, Reveren',' he apologized. 'Anyhow, it wouldn't seem right to call you by it.'

Caleb gave Pearl a kiss on the cheek and she gushed back to her chores, telling her husband to 'break out that bottle of whisky you've got hidden'. Aaron smiled and called his three children over.

The eldest was a girl aged about sixteen by the name of Elizabeth, the eldest son, about fourteen, was called Nathaniel and the youngest, a boy aged about ten, was known as Daniel. As ordered, Aaron produced the bottle of whisky and Caleb was pleased to see that it was a good Scotch brand. He was not a drinking man as a rule, but when he did have a drink, there was nothing he liked better than a good Scotch.

After the meal of spicy chicken and rice, which he thoroughly enjoyed, Caleb produced a couple of cigars and sat with Aaron on the front porch, away from the sight of the rubbish tip, sipping whisky and smoking.

'What do you know about Colonel George Baker?' the preacher suddenly asked.

Aaron looked rather alarmed and Caleb sensed that he had hit upon something of a delicate matter.

28

TWO

It was very unusual for the hands from the three large outlying ranches to hit town on a Sunday evening, but this particular Sunday, it seemed that almost every one of them had decided to ride in. From what Matt McCauley could ascertain, the interest appeared to be the presence of the rather strange preacher in their midst.

To most of them, the excuse of wanting to see the preacher was nothing more than that, an excuse. For them, the main preoccupation of the evening was to get drunk again. However, there were three or four, all from the Carter Ranch, who seemed hell bent on challenging a man who had suddenly acquired the reputation of being very good and very fast with a gun. These men were not true cowboys, they were hired primarily for their supposed skills with guns and their ability to kill or maim without question.

Having eventually managed to persuade Aaron Williams to tell everything he knew about Colonel George Baker, the Reverend Caleb Black made his way back to his lodgings with Ernie and Mary Stollard. The information he now had in his possession had started a train of thought which promised to be quite profitable, but to achieve that, he needed to reach Fort Benson, the army headquarters for the territory, which was apparently located some eighty miles due west.

The fact that there were so many ranch hands in town did not mean anything to Caleb, he had only arrived in Reno three days previously, so it did not appear strange. His approach, down the long, wide street, had been seen almost as soon as he left Aaron Williams' shack and as he drew nearer to the only saloon in town, he realized that it was he who was the main object of attention.

Most of the catcalls were directed at the colour of his skin, but he was used to that and it did not bother him all that much.

He had also become accustomed to men suddenly leaping out in front of him and challenging him in some way, although he had hoped that he might have left all that behind him. Therefore, he was not too surprised when two burly figures suddenly blocked his way.

'Well, now,' grinned one of them, a man he later learned was called Sven Olfsen. 'What's a black preacher doin' all the way out here?' He laughed coarsely. 'You oughta be back down south, convertin' all them heathen slaves I hear they've got down there.'

'I think my time would be better spent converting a few white heathens!' replied Caleb, well aware that he might be goading the men. 'Please excuse me.'

He tried to push past but, as he had expected, the men refused to be pushed. He smiled, nodded briefly and tried to walk round them, only to find them moving in front of him again.

'You've just come from the only place you oughta be,' laughed the other man, Clem Gordon. 'That's why that turd

31

Williams lives out there, folk like you an' him are only fit to live on rubbish heaps.'

'I have lodgings with the Stollards,' smiled Caleb. 'I have things I must attend to, please let me pass.'

'Please let me pass!' mimicked Clem Gordon. 'What the hell is any church thinkin' of, lettin' a black turd be a preacher?'

'Perhaps it's because there aren't enough white turds around to do the job!'

'Who the hell are you to call us turds?' yelled Sven Olfsen. 'I've killed men for less'n that!'

'I can believe it!' goaded Caleb, his hands slipping casually into the deep pockets of his frock coat.

At that moment, Sheriff Matt McCauley appeared behind the men and clamped a hand on their shoulders.

'What the hell is all this about?' he demanded. 'Sven, Clem, I guessed you were out to cause trouble. Now I'm tellin' you, either get out of town or go get yourself a drink, but I don't want to hear either of you causin' no more trouble.'

'We ain't causin' no trouble,' complained Clem Gordon, 'it was the Reverend here, he called us white turds an' we don't like that.'

'But it's OK for you to call him a black turd?' queried the sheriff. 'Don't mix words with me; I can just as easy find room for you in one of my cells for the night.'

'Nobody calls us turds!' hissed Sven Olfsen.

'Not even me?' laughed McCauley. 'The Reverend was right, you are both a couple of turds. Personally I'd rather see you out of my county altogether, you've been nothin' but trouble since you arrived. Now, do you spend the night in jail or what?'

Sven Olfsen shook the sheriff's hand off his shoulder and glared hatred at the preacher. 'Nobody calls me a turd an' gets away with it!' he threatened.

Both men grumbled their way towards the saloon and Matt McCauley ordered the expectant crowd to disperse and go about their business, which they did, slowly and grudgingly. Most of them felt that they had been denied some entertainment.

'There's two more reasons why it ain't too healthy for you to hang about town longer'n necessary,' he warned the preacher.

'I was ready for them,' said Caleb. 'A pity though, I had hoped things might be different out here. It seems I was wrong though, men still use colour as a means of causing trouble.'

'Don't take it that's how everyone is,' said Matt. 'Most just accept the colour of a man's skin an' treat them as bein' perfectly equal.'

'Even here?'

'Sure, what's that supposed to mean?'

'Aaron Williams,' said Caleb.

'Aaron?' queried Matt.

'Sure,' smiled Caleb. 'If all men are equal, why is it that Aaron cannot find work in what he does best? He's a blacksmith by trade, but he can't find work. He even tried setting up on his own, but there just wasn't enough trade to keep him going.'

'That's 'cos this town ain't big enough

to take two blacksmiths,' said Matt.

'The other blacksmith refused to hire Aaron, even though he knew he was good. Instead he chose to take on another untrained man who hardly knew one end of a horse from another. He told Aaron that he daren't hire him. If he did, he'd probably lose what business he had. Not only that, the Williams family are forced to live out almost on top of the tip; that can't be right can it? Aaron has to make his living cleaning soil pits.'

'Somebody's got to clean 'em!' Matt pointed out.

'You're right!' sighed Caleb. 'Perhaps I am expecting too much. However, I make note of your warning, Sheriff. I shall be on my way as soon as the money is cleared.'

Matt McCauley smiled and left the preacher to make his way back to his lodgings but Caleb had a sense of something being amiss before he reached the door.

'Er...er...Reverend,' faltered Ernie Stollard. 'I... er it's...'

The preacher smiled ruefully and nodded

his head. 'Don't tell me, you've been warned off lettin' me stay here!'

'Well... er... yeh, somethin' like that,' muttered a very embarrassed Ernie Stollard. 'If it was left to me, Reverend, you know I wouldn't...'

'I understand, Mr Stollard,' smiled Caleb, disarmingly. 'You don't have to worry about me, I'll find somewhere. Answer me one question though. Who made you do this?'

Ernie Stollard shuffled uneasily and stared at the ground. 'I can't say,' he whispered. 'Believe me, Reverend, I really can't say. It'd be more'n my life's worth.'

'Far be it from me to put anyone's life at risk,' said Caleb. 'I think I might have an idea who's behind it all though. I won't embarrass you any further, Mr Stollard, I'll just take my bag and leave you in peace.'

Mary Stollard, a plump, middle-aged woman, appeared behind her husband carrying the preacher's carpet bag, which she handed to him without looking at him.

'Everythin's in there,' she mumbled. 'Under the circumstances, we won't be askin' you for the cost of your board so far, it wouldn't seem right.'

'I thank you,' said Caleb, taking the bag. 'I am only sorry that things have turned out like this.'

'Us too,' choked Ernie Stollard. 'I was tellin' the truth when I said I didn't know who was behind it. All I know is we was warned off by the boys from the Carter Ranch. It don't do to argue with Carter nor his hired guns.'

'Perhaps I ought to pay this Carter a visit,' muttered Caleb.

'If you want to stay alive,' said Mary Stollard, 'I wouldn't go nowhere near him. He hates all blacks an' he only tolerates havin' Aaron Williams around 'cos there's nobody else to clean out the soil pits.'

'A powerful man it seems,' said Caleb. 'Men like him usually have something to hide, I wonder what his secret is?'

'He's powerful OK,' said Ernie. 'We don't ask any questions; that way at least, we get to stay alive.'

'Well, I thank you for all you have done for me,' said Caleb, raising his hat to Mary Stollard. 'Since it would seem that other folk are not about to offer me lodgings, I am quite certain that even the powerful Mr Carter could have no objections to my bedding down with the soil-pit cleaner.'

'I'd say that was about the only choice you've got,' agreed Ernie. 'I hope you don't think I...we...'

'I hold nothing against you,' interrupted Caleb. 'I can understand how you feel. Don't worry, this isn't the first time such a thing has happened to me. I shall survive it and I shall probably come across it again. Once again, I thank you for what you have done so far.' He raised his hat again and turned sharply.

Despite his outward appearance of calm, Caleb Black was seething beneath his preacher's garb. True, such things had happened to him before, several times, but it still made him very angry.

His route took him back past the saloon, where Sven Olfsen and Clem Gordon, along with several others, were lounging on the boardwalk, leering at the preacher as he deliberately gave them a wide berth. It was not that he was in any way afraid of them, on the contrary, he was quite confident that he could outgun any of them singly or even two of them, but at least six opponents was a different matter. They did not attempt to cause any trouble or stop him as he passed by, a fact probably helped by the presence of Matt McCauley standing at the front of his office.

Aaron Williams did not seem all that surprised to see the preacher back at his shack and Pearl fussed around, taking his bag and insisting that he must have the 'big bed behind the drapes'. Caleb knew that this was the bed Aaron and Pearl used and tried to object, pointing out that he had often had to sleep on floors or in barns, but neither Pearl nor Aaron would hear otherwise.

'Ah cain't say as I'm too surprised,' said Aaron when everything had been sorted out. 'Pity about the Stollards though; they're good folk, just like most of the folk in town, but they have to do what they're told, just like me. It don't pay to argue.'

'Does this Carter run the territory?' asked Caleb.

'Pretty well,' said Aaron. 'Most folk take their orders from him an' them that don't don't argue with him.'

'Does that include Sheriff McCauley?'

Aaron thought for a moment. 'No, Ah don't reckon it does. Mind you, he don't go out of his way to annoy Carter. 'Sides, Ah reckon Carter finds it useful to have a sheriff who don't take sides with nobody. Sort of good for his image. He accepts that his boys are just as likely to get arrested for bein' drunk as anyone else an' he pays their fines.'

'And Colonel George Baker?'

'Ah reckon he does as he's told,' said Aaron, 'although there's a sorta funny relationship between him an' Carter. It's almost as if Carter's scared of him in some way.'

'Interesting!' mused Caleb. 'Now, are you quite sure I'm not putting you out too much? I'll pay you for my keep, that's only fair. How about two dollars a night?'

'We don't want any money off you, Reverend!' objected Aaron, only to be glared at hard by his wife. Caleb did not miss the look and smiled at her.

'That's settled,' he laughed. 'Never argue with a woman; after all, it's her who has to do the cookin' and cleanin'.'

'Well, if it's OK by you, Reverend,' said Aaron apologetically. 'Ah guess we can allus use the money. Two dollars seems a lot though...'

Once again he was glared at by Pearl.

Having established where he was sleeping and the cost, Caleb announced that he was going to talk to the sheriff. Both Aaron and Pearl seemed rather alarmed.

'Reveren'!' warned Pearl. 'It just ain't wise to go down there, not with all them men from the ranches, 'specially that Sven Olfsen an' Clem Gordon. They only came in to cause trouble, they don't usually come in on a Sunday night.'

'I hear what you say,' smiled Caleb, 'but I have found that it just doesn't pay to give in to such men; all they do is take it as a sign of weakness and try and push you further. I've never run scared from any man yet and I don't intend to start now.'

'I still don't think it's wise,' insisted Pearl. 'Better be safe and alive than brash and dead.'

'Death is something we all have to face,' smiled Caleb. 'I have no fear of death, this life is but a passage to eternal peace and happiness.'

'Ah don't know 'bout that,' grunted Aaron. 'We ain't got book learnin' like you have. I for one ain't in no hurry to find out what the afterlife is like.'

'Don't get me wrong,' laughed Caleb, 'I'm not over anxious to find out what it's like either, but I ain't scared of it.'

'Ah guess you know your own mind!' sighed Aaron. 'If you gets yoursel' into trouble though, we can't help much, the only gun Ah own is an ancient muzzle loader; we have better things to spend our money on.'

'Very wise!' grunted Caleb, checking his

guns. 'Maybe I won't need these, I hope not, but just in case...'

The men lounging outside the saloon seemed rather surprised to see the preacher walking down the street and one of them rushed inside the saloon to return a minute later with two other men, Clem Gordon and Sven Olfsen. Neither man said a thing as the preacher passed them, walking down the centre of the street and then going across to the sheriff's office. Matt McCauley too seemed somewhat surprised to see him.

'Found yourself lodgings?' Matt asked.

'Of course!' replied Caleb. 'Not everyone has been warned off.'

'Who said anyone had been warned off?' queried Matt.

'The Stollards,' said Caleb. 'They made it plain enough they'd been warned off by those men, the ones from the Carter Ranch.'

'Sven Olfsen an' Clem Gordon,' Matt McCauley nodded.

'You seem to know all about it,' said Caleb.

'I ain't surprised, let's put it like that.'

'I thought you were the sheriff here, do you allow decent folk to be terrorized in this way?'

'I'd hardly call it bein' terrorized,' smiled Matt. 'Anyhow, as far as I know, there ain't no law been broken, therefore there ain't nothin' I can do. My job is to keep the peace an' the law, not act as nursemaid.'

'I might have guessed as much!' grumbled Caleb.

Matt laughed and lounged back in his chair, his hands folded across his chest. 'Look at it this way, Reverend,' he said. 'God an' the church, weddin's, christenin's an' funerals, they're all part of your business, there ain't nobody gonna argue with that. You know the Bible, I know the law, that's my business. You wouldn't expect me to hold services in your church, so I don't expect you to keep the peace an' the law. Like I said, as far as I know there ain't no laws been broken. Folk are free to put anyone up as payin' guests if they want or not, as they choose.'

'I take your point,' admitted Caleb, 'but there is a certain moral aspect that affects us all.'

'Morals ain't the law,' insisted Matt. 'I should've thought most preachers would've realized that.'

'So you don't intend to do anything about it?'

'It ain't a matter of wantin' to,' said Matt, 'it's simply a matter of not bein' able to. Sure, I could talk to Sven an' Clem an' maybe even to Carter, but they'd most likely just deny it an' then it'd be their word against the Stollards'. No, Reverend, my hands are tied. If they step out of line an' break the law, then maybe I can do somethin', but until they do, there ain't a thing I can or will do.'

'I thank you for being so frank,' said Caleb. 'Still, with luck, I shouldn't be around much longer to cause any annoyance. I'll just pick up my money and go.'

'It's a pity,' sighed Matt. 'This town could do with a regular preacher. I think most of 'em would accept you, no matter what colour your skin is.'

'I'd prefer a more welcoming atmosphere!' said Caleb. 'Now, perhaps you could answer me a couple of questions. How come this Carter is so powerful an' what connection is there between him and Colonel George Baker?'

Matt shrugged. 'Eli Carter is powerful simply 'cos he is. He's been here longer'n Reno, he was the first settler. In fact it was largely him who started this town. As for any connection between him an' George Baker... There ain't none that I know of, 'ceptin' they're good friends.'

'That all?'

'Sure, what else? You seem to have a bee in your bonnet about Colonel Baker. You made some wild claim about him not bein' who he says he is. OK, so maybe he is an' maybe he ain't, I can't say as I'm bothered one way or the other. All I know is the colonel is a good, upright citizen of Reno an' that's enough for me.'

'I have a little more than just a feeling,' said Caleb. 'My information is that Colonel Baker was brought here by someone, probably this Eli Carter, but that's not certain. My information is also that he brought with him a considerable amount of gold, which seems to have disappeared, or at least, is well hidden.'

'You've been talkin' to Aaron Williams!' laughed Matt. 'It ain't no secret, Aaron an' the colonel never did see eye to eye. Aaron reckons there was gold hidden in one of the soil pits, but when we looked we found nothin' but shit. Ever since then he's been tryin' to score points off the colonel.'

'I have a feeling there is more to it than that,' said Caleb. 'Yes, I have been talking to Aaron and he did tell me about the gold. He wouldn't tell me any more, but I had the feeling that there was more.'

'OK, so maybe there is,' said Matt. 'Whatever it is ain't nothin' to do with me. Anyhow, why all this interest? You said yourself that you'll be leavin' as soon as the money's passed.'

'I suppose you could put it down to idle curiosity,' smiled Caleb. 'Mysteries always intrigue me and I hate leaving with a mystery unsolved. I still say that Colonel

George Baker is not who he claims to be and I have a feeling that he knows I know. He's probably just hopin' I'll go away and leave him alone.'

'And shall you?'

'Very probably,' admitted Caleb, 'although, like I said, I don't like leavin' unsolved mysteries behind.'

'I'd say you would be makin' trouble for yourself if you tried to solve it,' said Matt. 'Me, I'm all for the easy life; I don't go lookin' for problems, I get enough of 'em comin' to me without botherin'. I'd've thought a preacher would've wanted an easy life too. One day's work a week don't seem too hard.'

'One day!' exclaimed Caleb. 'More like eight! That's the trouble with people like you. All you see is what we do in church on a Sunday an' maybe the odd weddin', christenin' or funeral in the week. I can assure you that there is a whole lot more to it than that. Not so much for me, travellin' about like I do, but a preacher with a permanent parish has a whole lot more to do.'

'That's why we need a regular preacher here,' smiled Matt. 'I know that, Reverend, I was only jestin'.'

'Were you?' The preacher sounded as though he did not really believe the sheriff. 'OK, maybe you were, it doesn't matter. Now, do you think this Carter or his men have told the bartender at the saloon that I am to be refused a drink?'

'Wouldn't know,' shrugged Matt. 'I wouldn't reckon so, they probably think preachers don't drink anyhow.' He looked severely at the preacher. 'What you wanna go in there for anyhow? You wouldn't be lookin' to stir up trouble would you?'

'I owe Aaron Williams a bottle of whiskey,' smiled Caleb. 'I just figured the saloon would be the most likely place to buy a bottle.'

'That sounds fair enough,' said Matt, suspiciously.

'Anyhow, Sheriff,' grinned Caleb, 'you just said you can't do anythin' if there is no law being broken. As far as I am aware, there is no law which bars a preacher from a saloon, not even a coloured preacher.

Leastways not in these parts, some of the southern States, maybe, but not here.'

'I guess you're right at that,' admitted Matt, 'but just you make sure you don't go causin' no trouble. I'll know the truth of it, no matter what you or anyone else says. The bartender just happens to be my brother!'

'And you would trust your brother?' laughed Caleb. 'I have a brother, older than me, and I would never have trusted him with anything. That was before I was ordained though and I reckon I'd trust him even less now.'

'That's where him an me are different from most brothers,' laughed Matt. 'I doubt if anyone, 'ceptin' maybe our wives, could tell us apart. Most folk just say, "Matt, he's the one with the badge"! We're twins, lookin' exactly the same. Sometimes I even think we can read each other's minds. I chose to become a sheriff, he decided to buy the saloon.'

'Thanks for warning me,' said Caleb. 'It could have come as something of a shock to have just left you and meet you again behind the counter.'

'Just remember,' warned Matt, 'I don't want to hear of you, preacher or not, startin' any trouble. Mick'll tell me if you do. I ain't never had a preacher in my jail before, but I guess there's always a first time.'

'The experience would not be new to me!' grinned Caleb.

'That, I can believe!' grunted Matt.

THREE

The saloon was full and noisy, but as Caleb Black pushed open the swing doors, all sounds suddenly ceased and all eyes turned to stare at the black-clad figure as he stopped, looked smilingly and casually about and then walked to a vacant space at the counter. Even Sven Olfsen and Clem Gordon looked stunned at the preacher's sudden appearance and seemed a little unsure of themselves.

All eyes were still on the preacher as Mick McCauley moved along the counter towards him, wiping away a pool of spilled beer as he did so.

'Reverend?' asked Mick McCauley, his voice booming in the almost graveyard silence. 'What can I do for you?'

'A bottle of your best Scotch whisky,' replied Caleb, apparently taking no notice of what was, or was not, happening about him.

In reality he was keeping a close check on any movements that were reflected in the large mirrors behind the bar. He did not miss Sven Olfsen and Clem Gordon detaching themselves from a crowd of other men and coming slowly in his direction.

'Best Scotch?' grunted Mick. 'That's out back, ten dollars a bottle.'

'Ten dollars?' smiled Caleb. 'That seems a little dear.'

'Ten dollars,' insisted Mick. 'I ain't takin' you for a ride, Reverend, it's ten dollars a bottle even if you was a tramp off the street or Eli Carter.'

'Your brother is right,' said Caleb. 'I wouldn't have been able to tell you apart, except for that small scar in the corner of your mouth.'

'Observant!' nodded Mick. 'Yeh, I got that in a fight last year. You're the first to notice it. OK, so me and Matt is alike as two peas in a pod. Ten dollars for the whisky. Are you still thinkin' of buyin'?'

'Provided it's the best Scotch, I'm still buyin'!'

'I'll go get it!' Mick disappeared and

54

immediately Caleb saw the two men closing in behind him.

'Blacks ain't allowed in this saloon!' grated Clem Gordon.

Caleb slowly turned and quite deliberately and rather pointedly, raised his hat to the two men. 'Good evening, brothers!' he greeted, knowing full well that such a greeting would not be appreciated by them. 'I did not see a notice to that effect as I came in.'

'There ain't no need for a notice,' rasped Olfsen. 'Everybody knows blacks ain't allowed in.'

'Do they?' smiled Caleb, leaning back against the counter. 'I don't, for one. Are you the owner of this establishment?'

'Don't come with no fancy big words!' snapped Clem Gordon.

'Big words?' queried Caleb. 'Oh, I see, you mean "owner"?' He could not help but goad the men.

'You know damned well what we mean!' rasped Olfsen again.

'I'm sure I don't,' grinned Caleb. 'I merely asked if either of you were the owner of this saloon?'

At that point the real owner of the saloon, Mick McCauley, returned with the whisky and gave the two men a withering, warning look.

'Ten dollars!' he demanded, holding his hand out.

'Mr McCauley,' said Caleb, not turning round, 'it would appear that you are breaking your own rules.'

'What are you talkin' about, Reverend?' sighed Mick, sensing that trouble was about to start.

'These two er...gentlemen have just informed me that black people are not allowed to be served in your saloon.'

'They would!' snapped Mick. 'Now look here, Reverend, take your whisky an' get out of here. I run an orderly saloon an' I won't allow either a preacher nor two hired guns to upset it. Just hand over your ten dollars an' go.'

'A beer!' smiled Caleb. 'I have suddenly developed a thirst and I do fancy a beer.'

'Reverend!' warned Mick, with a resigned sigh.

'A beer!' insisted Caleb.

He pulled a ten-dollar note out of his waistcoat pocket and handed it back to Mick McCauley, still without turning round. He took a fifty-cent piece from his trouser pocket and tossed that on to the counter.

'I warned you!' sighed Mick, although he did pull a small glass of beer and placed it alongside the preacher.

Caleb took the bottle of whisky and slipped it into his pocket and picked up the glass of beer, grimacing slightly. He was not a beer drinker, not really liking the taste, but at that moment that particular beer had a flavour all of its own.

Actually, Caleb felt rather disappointed; the two men had made no attempt to stop him or to say anything else to him, they simply stood and stared. There had been a slight resurgence of talk, but it had suddenly died down again. Caleb decided that he was not going to achieve anything else, so he drained his beer and started to leave. It was as he placed his glass on the counter that he saw the reason for the sudden silence and the reluctance of either Sven Olfsen or Clem Gordon to do anything. Mick McCauley and his assistant were both standing behind the counter with rifles aimed in their general direction.

'I see how you keep order!' Caleb laughed. 'Thank you, Mr McCauley, you keep quite a good beer; I hope the Scotch proves to be as good as the label claims it is.'

'It's the best!' snapped Mick. 'Imported straight from Scotland.'

Caleb smiled, patted the bottle in his pocket and raised his hat to the two men again. 'Farewell, brothers!' he said, moving round them and going to the door.

He knew they were behind him and he also knew that almost the entire clientele of the saloon had followed them out on to the street. Although it was well past sunset, there was plenty of light from the almost full moon and lights from various stores around. Caleb Black braced himself for action.

'I reckon you ought to be sharin' that

whisky!' rasped a voice, which Caleb recognized as belonging to Clem Gordon.

'I reckon whisky is wasted on blacks,' responded Sven Olfsen. 'They're just like the Indians, firewater they calls it; one sniff an' they is as drunk as they'll ever be. That's why the law says Indians can't buy whisky. I reckon it's probably the same for blacks, even black preachers.'

'Yeh, 'specially black preachers!' agreed Clem Gordon.

Caleb chose to ignore their remarks, but his pace slowed noticeably, he was ready for their next move.

'They tell me blacks got a sense of rhythm we ain't got,' said Olfsen. 'Can you dance, Reverend?'

'Let's find out,' laughed Clem Gordon.

Caleb could not actually see the dust rising from the two shots but he did feel and hear the bullets slam into the ground somewhere near his feet. He stopped, slowly turned around and simply stared at the two men. Several more shots raised dust around him, nowhere near his feet in actual fact and he smiled as he stood and waited—waited and counted...

'Nine, ten, eleven, twelve!' he said to himself. As the twelfth shot thudded into the ground, he drew both his Colts and laughed.

A fusillade of shots thudded into the ground very close to the feet of the two men, even singeing the leather of their boots. Sven Olfsen and Clem Gordon were suddenly dancing the jig they had tried to force the preacher into doing. Apart from a very few other men, the whole crowd laughed and even applauded the sight. Caleb stopped firing and grinned at the men.

'It would seem that you are far better at dancing than I am!' he called.

Olfsen held out his hand to one of his cronies and a gun was tossed to him, another gun was tossed to Clem Gordon. Both men snarled and slowly raised their new guns.

'Now you die!' rasped Gordon.

'Do I?' smiled Caleb, his guns held steadily at them. 'Did you count how many shots I fired? I know what you're thinkin', he's used all his bullets, but did I? Maybe I did, maybe I didn't. Before you take aim, think about it. How many shots did I fire? Was it twelve? Maybe it was only ten, one left for each of you.'

Clem Gordon looked at his companion and licked his lips in apprehension. Both men knew that by the time they had taken a sure aim on the preacher, his shooting was far more accurate than theirs and they could be dead. Their dilemma was solved for them as Sheriff McCauley ordered them to drop their guns.

'I warned you two!' grated McCauley. 'No trouble I said. That goes for you too, Reverend. I reckon a night in jail an' a heavy fine for disturbin' the peace wouldn't come amiss. Now move, the three of you. OK, folks, show's over!'

'The Reverend didn't do nothin'!' called a voice from the crowd. 'He was walkin' away. It was them two. By rights, the Reverend could've killed 'em!'

'He's right, Matt!' Mick McCauley stepped from the crowd. 'He didn't do nothin'. He came into my place, bought a ten-dollar bottle of whisky, had a glass of beer an' left. Olfsen an' Gordon tried to goad him in there, but he didn't have none of it. It was them who started it out here.'

Matt McCauley glared at Caleb and grunted. 'Seems you got most folk on your side, Reverend. OK, you can go, although I still think you could've avoided it all if you'd gone straight back. You two, I've got a nice cell all ready an' waitin'. Somebody can tell Carter you're here an' he can get you out in the mornin'. I reckon the Reverend an' the town will be a whole lot safer the quicker you're locked away. Now move!'

The men protested loudly, but they were taken away. The majority of the crowd gave Caleb a cheer as he turned and made his way back to the Williams' shack. The few who did not seem pleased ran for their horses and rode swiftly out of town.

Aaron and Pearl had heard the shooting and the relief at seeing the preacher enter their front door was very plain. Pearl fussed round, taking Caleb's coat and ushering him to the best chair.

'What you got in this pocket?' she laughed, tapping it.

'Whisky!' said Caleb. 'A bottle of the best Scotch. Since I drank most of yours this afternoon, I thought it only right to replace it. It's almost too dear to drink.'

'Hell, Reverend!' said Aaron. 'You needn't've done that. Pearl don't like me drinkin' that much an' havin' you around gave me a good excuse, even if she did suggest it.'

'That's 'cos you gets morbid an' stupid when you drinks by yourself,' scolded Pearl.

'Don't they allow you into the saloon?'

'Oh sure!' said Aaron. 'There ain't no problem there, despite folks like Eli Carter an' the colonel.'

'And thugs like Sven Olfsen and Clem Gordon?'

'Ah, don't go in there that often,' laughed Aaron. 'Ah ain't exactly popular durin' the day. The stench of shit sticks to everythin' the shit itself don't stick to. Ah never go in on Saturday night when the ranches are in town, it just ain't worth it. Ah goes in maybe once every two weeks, it's enough for me.'

'It should be enough for any man!' said Pearl, with more than a hint of derision. 'I've seen women with terrible black eyes an' swollen jaws on a Sunday mornin'. Saturday night is just about the most popular time for walkin' into doors an' things!' She laughed. 'One thing I'll say about Aaron, he ain't never lifted a hand to me yet.'

'Ah'll lift a hand to you, if you don't get the Reverend somethin' to eat!' laughed Aaron. 'Well, Reverend, since you've so kindly brought a new bottle of whisky, there don't seem that much point in keepin' what's left of the old bottle. What say we finally kill it off?'

There was no trouble during the night and, with Olfsen and Gordon safely locked away, Caleb had not really expected any. Monday was a normal working day and he thought that they would be too busy to bother about him and, with luck, the authorization for the reward would come through and he could be on his way.

To pass the time, Caleb went along to the blacksmith's stable where he had left his horse, just to be nosy and check that everything was all right. On the way, he saw the back end of Olfsen and Gordon, along with another man, riding away from town. If they had seen him, they did not show it.

'That was some fancy shootin', last night,' grinned the blacksmith. 'Maybe you didn't do yourself no favours though, them two is used to havin' their own way.'

'You mean they could cause more trouble?'

'I'd take bets on it,' the blacksmith grinned again. 'Maybe they won't do nothin' in town. Even if they wanted to, Eli Carter ain't stupid, he knows Matt'll run 'em in an' charge 'em with murder or somethin'. No, Reverend, I hear you're leavin' soon, all I can say is watch your back.'

'Thanks for the warning,' said Caleb. 'The thought had crossed my mind as well. Actually, I had thought of riding out to see this Eli Carter, he sounds a most interesting man.'

'I suppose you could say that!' grinned the blacksmith. 'He's got a lot of faults, ain't no denyin' that, but if it weren't for him, there's a whole lot of things wouldn't've happened in Reno that have. He started the town.'

'So I hear,' said Caleb. 'That's why I would like to meet him, I wonder what makes a man like that work.'

The blacksmith straightened his back and looked down the street. 'There ain't no need for you to ride out to his place, you can talk to him right here...'

He pointed at a man standing talking to Sheriff McCauley. 'That's him now.'

Caleb could see a tall, slender man, well dressed and without guns, which was not unusual for a man like him. It was not the done thing: he could afford hired guns to protect him.

Caleb raised his hat to the blacksmith and made his way towards the sheriff's office. The two men saw him approach,

66

Matt McCauley with a slight smile on his face and Eli Carter very grim-faced.

'Good morning, Sheriff, Mr Carter,' greeted Caleb, once again raising his hat. 'Nice to meet you at last, Mr Carter, I've been hearing a lot about you.'

'Not as much as I've been hearin' about you!' grunted Carter. 'You just cost me twenty dollars.'

'I just cost you twenty dollars?' smiled Caleb. 'How can that be so, Mr Carter? I am certain that I have done nothing to incur any expense to you.'

'Sven was right!' growled Carter. 'You talk very grand an' flowery. You know darned well what I mean: it's just cost me twenty dollars in fines to get Sven an' Clem released.'

'That was hardly my doing,' said Caleb. 'They chose to pick a fight with me, I certainly did nothing to encourage them. I do believe there must be at least thirty witnesses to that effect.'

'Yeh, well, OK, maybe they did,' grumbled Carter. 'They tell me you're mighty handy with them guns of yours; I heard how you killed them three outlaws in the church. That's what bugs me about you, a preacher who wears two guns. I only ever met one man before who wore two guns. He was good, 'ceptin' his guns weren't good enough to stop a bunch of renegade Indians killin' him with an arrow.'

'Then I shall have to make sure I don't meet any renegade Indians,' smiled Caleb.

'About last night,' said Matt McCauley. 'I heard what you said about them countin' the shots you'd taken at them. Did you really have any bullets left?'

Caleb laughed and shook his head. 'That's one thing neither you nor they will ever know, Sheriff!' He turned his attention to Eli Carter. 'I hear that you and Colonel George Baker are very friendly; do you go back to army days together?'

'What the hell has anythin' like that got to do with you?' exclaimed Carter.

'Nothing at all, I suppose,' admitted Caleb. 'It's just that I am an old cavalry man myself. I was a lieutenant.'

'So what?' demanded Carter. 'You weren't the only black officer.'

'No, there were others,' agreed Caleb. 'It's just that I spent a couple of weeks with the Fifth Cavalry, the one Colonel Baker was supposed to be commanding officer of...'

'What you mean, supposed to be?'

'Oh, indeed Colonel Baker was the commanding officer,' smiled Caleb. 'The only thing is, your Colonel George Baker and the Colonel George Baker who was commanding officer of the Fifth, are not the same man.'

'You don't know what you're talkin' about!' hissed Carter.

'It took me a little time to be quite certain,' said Caleb, 'but I can assure you, even though I only met the man briefly, the man who lives here, claiming to be Colonel Baker, is not.'

'Look here, Reverend,' sighed Eli Carter, 'I don't know what all this is about or what the hell you're talkin' about and, to be perfectly honest, I couldn't give a damn who or what George Baker is or was. He's

69

a good citizen of Reno an' that's all that matters as far as I'm concerned an' I'm sure that goes for the sheriff an' everyone else in town.'

'Probably you're right,' smiled Caleb. 'I don't suppose for one moment that it matters at all. It was nothing more than idle curiosity. A man is bound to be curious if he knows something like that. I'm sure you would be.'

'Well I ain't!' snarled Carter. 'Now, I've got far better things to do than stand jawin' with a black preacher!' He nodded at Matt McCauley and ignored Caleb as he marched off along the boardwalk, his heavy tread clattering noisily.

'What the hell did you want to bring that up for?' demanded the sheriff. 'It seems to me you're hell-bent on causin' trouble in this town. Why, what's it done to you?'

'Hell-bent is hardly the correct term in my case,' laughed Caleb. 'Hell is a place I preach against. I'm sorry if I've upset your nice little town, Sheriff. If that money has been cleared, I can take it and be on my way and you may never hear of me again.'

'I'll go check at the telegraph office!' sighed Matt. 'I sure hope it's through soon, I've just about had my fill of you.'

Matt McCauley marched off towards the telegraph office and Caleb studied the contents of the window of the general store, the drapery store and even the corn and seed merchant. About ten minutes later, he heard Matt McCauley calling him and turned to see him waving a piece of paper.

'It's through!' yelled McCauley.

Caleb smiled and wandered over to the sheriff's office, where Matt showed him the message.

'All we've got to do now is draw the money from the bank. I know there's a wire for the bank as well. We'll give 'em ten minutes an' then go over. In the meantime, I'll just get you to sign these papers sayin' you've been paid...'

'I sign nothing until I have counted the money,' said Caleb. 'I was caught out like that once, only once. I signed the paper just like you said and the next thing I knew I was being run out of town. The sheriff and the bank president both swore they'd handed the money over to me and they produced the paper with my signature on it to prove it.'

'Didn't nobody believe you?'

'In Texas, who would ever believe the word of a black man?' said Caleb. 'There was absolutely nothing I could do.'

'OK,' smiled Matt, 'can't say as I blame you after that. C'mon, we'll go over to the bank: they should've had their wire by now.'

The president of the bank was a fussy little man, who had to have every piece of paper in exactly the right place and he seemed to object to paying out the money in his safe. However, after counting a wad of notes carefully for himself three times, he finally invited the preacher to count it.

'I take it you can count?' he asked. 'I would assume so, since you are a preacher.'

'I can count,' smiled Caleb. 'I can write too, even big words!' He was being sarcastic, but his sarcasm appeared lost on the fussy little man.

Caleb took his time and counted the notes, the first time making it ten dollars short, but on the second count his tally agreed with what it was supposed to be, $1,200. He signed three pieces of paper, one for the sheriff and two for the bank and left feeling quite satisfied.

He returned to the stable and saddled his horse, paid his bill and rode back to the Williams' shack, where he was met by Aaron.

'From the look on your face,' said Aaron, 'Ah'd say you was goin' on your way.'

'I've been paid,' said Caleb. 'I've just come to collect my things and thank you for your hospitality.'

'The pleasure was all ours, Reveren',' assured Aaron. 'You just make sure you call on us any time you is passin'.'

'I will,' said Caleb. He sniffed the air and smiled. 'I can see why you are not popular in the saloon during the day!' He wrinkled his nose.

'I guess we get used to it,' laughed Pearl,

coming out with the preacher's carpet bag. 'Now don't you go squashin' that bag too much, Reverend, I put some goodies inside to help you on your way.'

'I thank you, Pearl,' Caleb smiled. He gave her a kiss on the cheek and slipped something into her hand. She did not look at it until he had ridden away.

The Reverend Caleb Black rode slowly down the wide street of Reno, briefly acknowledged two passing ladies and then Sheriff Matt McCauley, at least he thought it was Matt McCauley, he had not noticed the badge of office. He smiled, he was usually quite certain about things, but that was one thing he could not be certain of, not that it mattered at all.

Pearl Williams watched the preacher disappear from view before she opened her hand. In it was what appeared to be a crumpled note. She slowly unfolded it and gasped.

'Aaron! Look at this...fifty dollars!'

It had been many a year since either Aaron Williams or his wife had seen so much money all at once.

FOUR

Caleb was well aware that he had stirred up something at least one citizen of Reno would rather not have had raised, but he was not too sure what action anyone was going to take. It was more than likely that they would choose to ignore what they considered to be the ramblings of a Negro preacher, especially since that preacher had now left town.

However, the Reverend Caleb Black was also only too well aware of the twists and turns of the human brain, especially when that brain perceived a threat against it. So, with that thought in mind, he rode fairly slowly and made frequent stops to check if he was being followed or not. For the first three hours, it seemed that he was not being followed and he began to wonder if he was being a little over-cautious.

The trail entered a canyon, not a very

wide or deep one, but there was no alternative but to descend into the canyon. It was as he edged his way down the steep, narrow trail, that he felt the feeling of unease. He had seen nothing and had heard nothing, but he did experience an almost overpowering sense of danger ahead.

The trail levelled off some ten or fifteen feet above a swirling river in the canyon bottom and continued for about a mile before reaching a small ford. At that point the trail divided, one leg continuing along the canyon bottom, following the river downstream and the other crossing and disappearing behind some large boulders to reappear further up the steep sides and twisting its way to the top.

The sign was quite clear; Fort Benson lay on the trail across the river. He looked at the rocks and boulders and still had the distinct feeling that he was about to ride into trouble and, for a moment, he seriously considered forgetting all about Colonel George Baker and Eli Carter. However, he was also quite certain that the Colonel George Baker of Reno and the Colonel George Baker of the Fifth Cavalry were not the same man and he had the feeling that there could well be a sizeable reward if the fact could be proved.

Unfastening the buttons of his long frock coat and easing his guns in their holsters slightly he urged his horse slowly across the river. He also casually unfastened the strap on his saddle holster, freeing his Winchester.

Once across the river, he was quickly amongst the boulders where the trail twisted and turned sharply as it climbed quite steeply. It was as he twisted around one large boulder that he caught a glimpse of the faintest of movements on the top of a large boulder directly ahead. It was possible that the movement had been caused by something like a large lizard or even a wild goat, but he did not think so.

On the pretext of checking the hoof of his horse, Caleb dismounted and picked up the forefoot of the animal. His eyes scanned the way ahead, looking for other tell-tale signs, but he could see nothing. As he let the hoof drop, his keen ears caught the sound of an animal snort, which he had to assume was a horse. He pretended he had heard nothing and led his horse back towards the river where, for the sake of anyone watching, he examined the hoof again.

Once again his careful study of the terrain did not reveal anything but he was still convinced that danger lay ahead. His horse was allowed to graze on a small patch of grass and he idly slipped his Winchester from the saddle holster and returned to the shade of a large rock, out of view of anyone up the trail.

The Reverend Caleb Black was a patient man and, since he had nowhere in particular to go and any amount of time in which to get to his one possible destination of Fort Benson, he settled down and waited...

It must have been about half an hour later that Caleb heard the distinct sounds of someone moving amongst the rocks on foot. There were the faintest scrapes as bootleather slipped on smooth rock and the occasional dislodged stone as an unwary foot came down a little too heavy.

'Where the hell is he?' came a whispered demand. 'His horse is there, so he can't be far away?'

'Could be anywhere,' whispered another voice. 'You look over there, I'll look down here!'

'There doesn't seem much point in either of you looking anywhere,' grated Caleb from the top of a large boulder, his rifle aimed at the two men. 'I was beginning to wonder when you two would show up. OK, drop those guns, real slow. If you don't, I might just happen to squeeze this trigger.'

'Bastard!' hissed Clem Gordon. 'How the hell did you know we were here?'

'I just guessed!' laughed Caleb. 'And I must correct you on your reference to my birth, my mother and father were married.'

'That don't make no difference to the fact they spawned a bastard!' rasped Sven Olfsen. 'OK, Mr Smart-Guy Preacher, you've got the draw on us for the moment an' we've dropped our guns. You can't stay up there for ever, you've gotta come down sometime.'

They had a point, Caleb was forced to admit and the only way down would take him out of their sight and they would be able to recover their guns. He thought about it for a moment and then raised his rifle again.

The echoes of gunfire rang around the canyon as Caleb fired at their guns, sending first one and the other skidding across the dusty earth and into the river.

'I guess I'll just have to take a chance as to whether your guns work,' he called, rapidly disappearing from view.

The two men raced to the water to recover their guns and had just done so when Caleb appeared again. Sven Olfsen tried firing his, but all he could get out of it was a click as the hammer slammed down. Clem Gordon had a little more success and a bullet ricocheted off a rock by his head. Clem did not have the chance of a second shot.

Caleb's shot in reply, thudded into Clem's shoulder, forcing him to drop the gun into the water. Sven tried again, with the same result as before and grinned ruefully, slowly dropping his gun alongside that of his companion.

'OK, Preacher!' taunted Sven. 'Now what are you goin' to do, kill us both?'

'I ought to,' grated Caleb, 'but I reckon neither of you can do much now.' He moved forward, drawing one of his Colts. 'Now, just what the hell is all this about? I can't believe that you tried to ambush me just 'cos of what happened in Reno.'

'We might've done anyhow,' hissed Clem Gordon, trying to stem the flow of blood from his shoulder with a handkerchief. 'We didn't though. It looks like somebody don't like you.'

'Eli Carter an' Colonel Baker?' suggested Caleb.

'Right on both counts!' nodded Sven Olfsen. 'We were told to ride out here an' kill you. We would've done too, 'ceptin' for that horse of yours goin' lame.'

'Yes, lucky that, wasn't it?' sneered

Caleb. 'How did you know I'd be comin' this way though?'

Sven Olfsen laughed. 'There ain't no other way you could've come. There's only one way across the canyon.'

'I could have carried on along the other side of the river,' Caleb pointed out.

'Yeh, maybe you could've,' agreed Sven. 'That was a chance we had to take an' we chose right.'

'Unluckily for you!' smiled Caleb. 'Now you can just get back to your master an' tell him what happened. I'm sure he won't be too pleased with you.'

Sven shrugged. 'It don't matter to us. Carter needs us, so he can rant an' rave all he wants.'

'So why should either he or Baker want me dead?'

'We weren't told an' we don't ask,' grated Clem Gordon, shuffling from the river, his arm hanging limply. 'Right now I agree with whatever reason they've got!'

'Things could've been worse!' laughed Caleb. 'I almost killed you. I think I need some more practice, I should have chewed

82

up that gun. It seems I was successful with yours though, Mr Olfsen. Yes, I know your names, I made it my business to find out.'

'An' we knows yours, Mr Caleb Black!' snarled Clem. 'I've got a long memory for names, especially folk I don't like.'

'That's interesting,' smiled Caleb. 'Why should you dislike me? Apart from just having shot you in the shoulder, what did I ever do to you? I certainly can't think of anything.'

'You shot my buddy!' grated Clem.

'I shot your buddy?' asked Caleb, a little mystified.

'Mick Fingerman—Fingers Mick!' hissed Clem. 'Me an' him went back a long way. I don't like it when folk kill friends of mine, 'specially someone like you.'

'Then you should be more careful in the choice of your friends!' grinned Caleb. 'Now I'll get on my way. I guess your horses are up there somewhere, so you can just wait here until I'm well away.'

'You'll never be able to run far enough!' scorned Sven Olfsen.

'Maybe, maybe not,' said Caleb with a shrug.

He went over to his horse and mounted and smiled slightly as both men realized they had been deceived.

'That horse ain't lame!' muttered Clem Gordon.

'I never said it was,' grinned Caleb. 'You just assumed it was and I didn't bother to correct you. Now, remember what I said, tell Carter and Baker what happened and how I chose not to kill you. I have the feeling I could have done quite legally; I'm sure there must be a reward out on you both somewhere.'

'Not in this State there ain't!' muttered Olfsen.

'But you have just confirmed that there is in some other State!' laughed Caleb. 'I won't bother though, you'd be more trouble than you are probably worth.'

He spurred his horse forward and disappeared amongst the rocks and boulders, his laughter echoing around the canyon. He found their horses about fifty yards up the trail and was tempted to herd them ahead of him, but he finally satisfied himself with simply cutting the straps of the saddles, which would mean Sven and Clem would have to ride bareback, thus delaying them even further.

As Caleb reached the top of the canyon, he looked back and saw the two looking dismally at their saddles and then staring hard at him. He gave them a wave and disappeared from view.

After half an hour of steady riding, Caleb came upon an isolated shack which, in actual fact, turned out to be a trading post, although it seemed to have precious little to trade. Caleb stopped briefly to ask the way to Fort Benson, since there were two trails leading away. He discovered that one commodity that was traded was information. For one dollar he was informed that the left-hand trail led to Fort Benson. The information as to how far Fort Benson was, cost him another dollar. Apart from having to pay two dollars to learn that Fort Benson was 'somethin' like eighty miles'—which made it seem that he had moved no nearer since leaving Reno—he was offered the services of the proprietor's wife for a further two dollars, with the assurance that she didn't mind takin' blacks or preachers. Caleb smiled and declined the offer.

'Do you know anything about a man called Eli Carter and a man called Colonel George Baker?' he asked again.

'That's two lots of information,' grunted the dirty, evil-smelling man. 'That kinda information don't come cheap either.'

'How much?'

'Ten dollars!' grated the man.

'Five dollars each question.' said Caleb, more to himself than to the proprietor.

'Ten dollars each question!' muttered the man.

Caleb laughed loudly. 'My need for the information is not that great. I'll give you a dollar each question.'

'Five!' haggled the man, sensing valuable money slipping away.

They eventually settled on five dollars for the two questions, with the proviso that Caleb considered the answers worth the money.

'Eli Carter,' rasped the man, eyeing the five-dollar note held tightly between Caleb's fingers. 'He's been here longer'n anyone, bar me an' my wife; we settled here when the Indians was still about. Ruined my trade he did, buildin' that town. 'Fore he came here, I hear tell that he was a quartermaster in the army...'

'Which unit?' urged Caleb.

'That I don't know,' admitted the man. 'All I know is there was some suspicion that he was helpin' himself to stores an' things from the army. I hear they couldn't prove nothin' though.'

'How do you know all this?' asked Caleb.

'I keep my eyes an' ears open,' said the man, who turned out to be called Zac Sheffield. 'In the early days there was an army major investigatin' him, but he never found nothin'.'

'And Colonel George Baker?' prompted Caleb.

'Don't know that much about him,' said Zac. 'He just sorta turned up. It was said that he had a hoard of gold bullion with him, but that was just rumour I reckon. Mind you, there was an army officer investigatin' Baker too, but I didn't hear nothin' about what he found, if he found anythin'.'

There it was again, gold bullion. Aaron Williams had sworn that he had seen some gold bars in a cesspit, but none had ever been found. Caleb felt that there must be something in the story and if there was gold bullion involved, it could make him a very wealthy man at even one tenth the likely value.

'I thank you,' said Caleb, giving the man the five dollars. 'I'd say it was well worth the money. Now, how would you like to earn yourself another ten dollars?'

'Who've I gotta kill for that money?' laughed Zac.

'Nobody,' assured Caleb. 'All you have to do is tell a lie, and I am quite certain that that would not cause you much of a problem.'

'Lie! What kinda lie?'

'It is quite possible that I may be being followed by at least two men from Eli

Carter's ranch. All you have to do is tell them I took the right-hand trail and not the left.'

'Easy enough,' grinned Zac. 'I'm allus gettin' confused with left an' right anyhow. Who are these guys?'

'Probably a man known as Sven Olfsen and possibly...'

'Clem Gordon!' hissed Zac, spitting venomously into the dust. 'Sure, I know 'em but I hope they don't head this way 'cos it'll take all of my will-power not to kill 'em.'

'I take it there is no love lost between you and them!' laughed Caleb. 'Whether you kill them or not is entirely up to you, although as a preacher I should tell you not to consider such a thing. All I want you to do is tell them I went along the other trail.'

'You got it, Reverend!' grinned Zac. 'Sure you don't want my woman? I reckon even preachers is human. You can have her free of charge, I can't say fairer'n that.'

'A fair price I would say,' grinned Caleb,

doffing his hat to the woman. 'But no, thank you.'

The woman grinned sheepishly and hurried into a dingy looking kitchen where she clattered some pans and plates about.

Feeling reasonably certain that Zac would keep his end of the bargain, Caleb set off once again for Fort Benson where, he was quite certain, they would know a lot more about Eli Carter and Colonel George Baker, particularly Colonel Baker.

'Well I reckon it was just plain stupid!' These words of condemnation came from the scowling figure of Colonel George Baker as he sat opposite Eli Carter in the comfort of the sitting-room at the Carters' ranch. 'All you've succeeded in doin' is makin' him suspicious.'

'He seemed to know too much,' defended Eli Carter. 'He reckoned he met the real Colonel Baker.'

'So what?' snarled Baker. 'He couldn't prove a thing; besides what if he could, there ain't no law against any man callin' himself what the hell he wants.'

'Maybe not,' agreed Carter. 'I ain't so sure about givin' yourself a rank you ain't entitled to though.'

'Same thing,' insisted Baker. 'Anyhow, Baker is my real name, Benjamin George Baker, an' I was in the Fifth Cavalry.'

'A corporal in the quartermaster's office ain't exactly the same as bein' colonel though.'

'You did well enough out of me,' hissed Baker. "Sides, after we killed the colonel, it seemed a waste not to keep drawin' his pension. He sure didn't need it an' I'd forged his signature so many times it was almost like my own.'

'All the more reason this preacher should be stopped,' insisted Carter. 'He could just convince somebody.'

'They've sent two investigators,' reminded Baker, 'an' neither of them could prove a thing.'

'But they weren't investigatin' you, not as to whether you was Colonel Baker or not, they were lookin' into the disappearance of the gold.'

'Only 'cos the colonel's signature was

on a shipment order,' said Baker. 'They seemed happy enough with what I told them.'

'That Captain Wells seemed a bit doubtful.'

'Facts!' laughed Baker. 'All the army is interested in is facts. No man is allowed to have opinions, not even captains an' colonels. If somethin' can't be backed up by facts, the army can't do nothin'. They can't 'cos they aren't trained that way; the system don't allow it.'

'You could be right,' sighed Carter. 'I just hope so. I still think that preacher's a danger though an' I've already sent Sven an' Clem out after him. With a bit of luck he'll be dead now.'

Baker nodded towards the window. 'Lookin' at the way those two are actin', I'd say he was still very much alive!'

Sven Olfsen and Clem Gordon could be seen heading towards the house, Clem Gordon's arm now in a sling. Carter rose and went to meet them at the door. Baker remained where he was as the two men explained, in hushed voices, that the Reverend Caleb Black was still very much alive. Carter barked an order at them and slammed the door in their faces. He was red-faced and very agitated when he returned to face Baker.

'Useless scum bags!' he hissed, venomously. 'They're supposed to be among the best there is when it comes to guns, but if they're the best then I'd be just as well off with a couple of blind cripples.'

'He got away!' smiled Baker.

'Yeh!' snarled Carter. 'Once is bad enough, but twice... They were made to look fools out in the street. All I can say is it's a damned good job nobody saw 'em out there.'

'What happened?' asked Baker.

'They reckon he was waitin' for 'em, somethin' about his horse goin' lame an' then not bein' lame! I don't know an' I don't care. Gordon's in no fit state to go after him again, so I've told Sven to take a couple of the others an' go out again. I also told 'em that if they couldn't do the job properly this time, they might just as well keep on ridin'!'

'I still think it was a stupid idea,' sighed Baker. 'I was all for just lettin' the preacher have his say, think whatever he wanted to think an' go on his way. After all, he did us a favour in gettin' rid of Fingers, Gibson and Ellison.'

'I won't disagree with that,' nodded Carter, 'but I think there's more to that particular preacher than it seems. For a start, how many preachers have you come across who carry one gun, let alone two, an' this preacher sure seems to know how to use both of 'em?'

'I suppose he is something rather different. I did meet one preacher who used a gun, but I'm still not sure if he did it for effect, so's he'd get more folk to listen to him, or for some other reason.'

'McCauley reckons he's really a bounty hunter,' said Carter. 'He is a proper preacher though; he showed McCauley a piece of paper provin' it.'

'A piece of paper doesn't prove a thing!' objected Baker. 'I have a paper proving I'm the real Colonel Baker.'

'There was an address on it,' said Carter.

'He pretended he wasn't interested, but he wired the address and, sure enough, the Reverend Caleb Black fits the description of the Caleb Black they know. They also said he was somethin' of a maverick and had been known to kill when it suited him.'

'It still doesn't prove a thing,' said Baker. 'Anyone could wire the army an' ask about me. I look near enough like Colonel Baker to fool anyone 'ceptin' someone who'd been very close to him. Why do you think I moved out here? Less chance of meetin' anyone who'd known him. Not even any of the soldiers or officers at the army post at Fort Benson would have served with him; they're engineers, he was cavalry. Even so, I have to act the part when I'm out, just in case.'

'I don't suppose anyone would want to impersonate a preacher,' laughed Carter, 'especially a black preacher. Most blacks ain't that well educated an' them that are wouldn't have a need to pretend they were someone else. No, he's preacher all right, a dangerous one at that. I still say we've got to get rid of him.'

'Suit yourself!' shrugged Baker. 'There's nothin' I can do about it now anyhow.'

Eli Carter looked out of the window as the sudden noise of hoof beats echoed around. He smiled wryly; Sven Olfsen had ridden out with three other men.

'Seems like Clem Gordon don't want to stay behind,' said Carter. 'He's just ridden out with Sven, Adam Smith an' Jake Evans.'

'Then I hope they have better luck than last time!' sneered Baker. 'Somehow I have this feelin' that you've just opened a can of worms that would've been better left alone.'

'Don't worry about them four, they're all good men.'

Baker laughed derisively. 'You said that about just Sven and Clem an' look what happened to them. I wish I had your faith, Eli. You just said you might be just as well off with blind cripples.'

Eli Carter scowled and stomped across to a cabinet where he poured himself a large whisky. He did not bother to offer one to his companion, simply indicating the bottle and then going to the window, where he stared moodily across the flat plain.

FIVE

'OK, so which way did he go?' Sven Olfsen demanded as the four riders sat menacingly astride their horses facing Zac Sheffield and his wife.

'Which way'd who go?' replied Zac, chewing on a wad of tobacco and spitting an evil-looking liquid on to the ground directly in front of Sven's horse. Even the horse seemed to object and shied slightly.

'How many travellers you had this way in the past two days?' sneered Clem Gordon.

Zac appeared to think about this for a moment before replying.

'Just one, I guess,' he finally admitted, without offering any further information.

'A black preacher name of Caleb Black,' said Sven.

Again Zac had to consider the question. 'I guess you could say he was a preacher;

he dressed like one anyhow, 'ceptin' I ain't never seen no preacher carryin' two guns afore. Come to think of it I ain't never seen a preacher who carried one gun. Come to think of it too, I ain't seen a preacher in the last ten years.'

'An' I bet you ain't never seen a black preacher before,' sneered Adam Smith.

'I only ever seen one black man before,' admitted Zac, 'an' that was the one you got in Reno, Aaron Williams.'

'OK, so now you've seen two,' grated Jake Evans. 'Which way'd this other one go?'

Once again Zac appeared to have a think about the question, made a couple of vague movements with his hands and arms and eventually announced 'Right! Yeh, that's the way. He took the right-and trail out towards Hawkesville.'

The four men looked at each other, unsure whether to believe Zac or not. Hawkesville was about 120 miles, whereas Benson and Fort Benson were only about eighty.

'What the hell did he go that way for?'

demanded Sven. 'Nobody ever wants to go to Hawkesville.'

'How should I know?' laughed Zac. 'He didn't even stop. All he did was say somethin' like "greetin's brother" an' just kept on ridin'. I know he took the trail to Hawkesville, 'cos, I stood an' watched him. I thought maybe he'd want somethin' to eat or maybe my woman, but he didn't seem interested in either.'

'Can't say as I blame him for not wantin' to chance your food!' laughed Jake Evans, looking leeringly at Zac's wife.

'Two dollars!' said Zac, seeing the look.

'She ain't worth two cents!' hissed Sven. 'OK, Zac, we're goin' after that damned preacher, but if he didn't take the trail you said, we'll come back an' when we do, neither you nor that woman of yours is gonna be worth two cents.'

'He went that way OK,' assured Zac. 'You'll have to move pretty fast though, he's more'n like up in Payute Mesa by now an' you must know once anyone's up there they could get lost for years.'

'I don't reckon he'll choose to stay up

there,' said Sven. 'OK, let's go. I've got me two scores to settle with that bastard of a preacher now, an' I aim to collect.'

Zac watched them ride out and smiled to himself. Probably for the first time in his life, Zac Sheffield had told the truth—or at least as near the truth as he was ever likely to get. He turned to his wife and laughed lightly.

'Best get all our guns loaded an' primed. It could be we is gonna be needin' 'em.'

Caleb made camp for the night alongside a small, clear stream which had a convenient hollow into a large rock alongside it. It could hardly be called a cave, but it did offer shelter from the cold evening wind which cut across the plain.

He estimated that he had travelled about thirty miles since leaving Reno, which still made Fort Benson about another fifty or more miles. It did not bother him particularly, but he would have liked to have reached Fort Benson as early as he could, especially since he had the feeling that already someone was on his trail.

He climbed to the top of the rock, which gave him quite an extensive view across the plain, although in the dying light it was difficult to see much and riders would have been almost impossible to spot.

However, he was reasonably satisfied that it would be most unlikely that anyone would have made that much time on him and he felt reasonably safe for the night.

It was just about the same time that Sven Olfsen decided that he had been sent off along the wrong trail. He and his men also made camp alongside a small stream although, unlike Caleb, they had not come prepared to stay out too long. None of them had even thought about food and, apart from a futile attempt at catching a fish, they had to resign themselves to going hungry.

It was suggested that one of them would ride back to Zac Sheffield's trading post, but since that was over five hours away, the idea was dropped.

It appeared that Adam Smith knew the territory fairly well and he drew a rough map in the dust. 'This is Reno,' he said, prodding a stick into the dust and making a small round mark. He drew the stick along, making a groove. 'This is the trail to Benson...' He drew another line off this one. 'This is the trail we're on. I'd say we was about here, I reckon we oughta strike the other' trail no more'n twenty or thirty miles from Benson.'

'How far?' demanded Sven.

'Oh, maybe fifty miles or thereabouts,' said Smith.

'Plus say thirty to Benson, that makes about eighty. Even ridin' hard that's gonna take two days, probably three.'

'So?' queried Smith.

'So, just what the hell do we eat between now an' then?' sneered Sven. 'It may have escaped your notice, but we ain't exactly equipped for this kind of thing.'

'You should've thought about that 'fore we left,' said Jake Evans.

'So should you!' sneered Sven.

'Not so!' objected Jake. 'All I did was obey orders an' get my butt out of the ranch an' follow you. You never said nothin' about what it was all about nor where we was goin'.'

'Quit gripin' at each other, you two!' snarled Clem Gordon. 'We ain't got no food. So what? We're all overweight anyhow, starvin' a couple of days'll do us good.'

Sven Olfsen and Jake Evans scowled at each other, but let the subject drop.

'Anyhow,' said Jake, eventually, 'why can't we just cut across north-west an' head straight for Benson?'

'Yeh,' agreed Sven. 'That way we might just get to Benson ahead of the preacher.'

Adam Smith smiled and drew two more lines in the dust, cutting across from the west to east. 'Canyon!' he announced. 'Unless you is ridin' mountain goats, there ain't no way down nor up. They do say the sides drop sheer for over two thousand feet an' the canyon goes on for more'n five hundred miles.'

Jake Evans whistled. 'Man! That must be some sight to see. I've heard of things like that, but I ain't never seen nothin' like it.'

'OK,' said Sven. 'So if this canyon is so deep an' Benson is the other side of it from here. Just how the hell do we get across?'

'Ferry!' said Smith. 'Leastways that's the way it used to be. There is one way down the canyon an' someone put a ferry across the river. Apart from that, I reckon it would mean a ride of another two or three hundred miles.'

'Same thing goes for the preacher too,' reminded Clem Gordon.

The same thing did go for the preacher. Caleb finally reached the bottom of the canyon, just in time to see the rickety looking ferry sailing away from his bank taking a covered wagon across the rough, muddy waters. Despite his shouting and calling, the ferryman resolutely refused to even acknowledge him.

It had taken him two days since first camping by the stream to reach this point and a sign had indicated that Benson and Fort Benson were only another fifteen miles the other side of the canyon, a couple of hours riding at most. He settled down to wait for the return of the ferry.

'Well now!' grinned Sven Olfsen, pointing down into the canyon. 'Looksee who I see down there!' He handed the spyglass he was using to Clem Gordon.

'The Reverend Caleb Black!' hissed Clem. 'He's waitin' for the ferry. Look, it's almost on the other side. Can we get down there 'fore it gets back?'

Sven and Clem looked at Adam Smith, who took the spyglass and looked through it. 'Might just about be able to,' he eventually agreed. 'It'll be cuttin' it pretty fine though. It depends on how long the ferry stays on the other side, but it sure don't look like there's anyone waitin', so he'll more'n like head straight back.'

'Then what the hell are we just sittin' here for?' barked Sven. 'Let's go get the bastard!'

The ferry did head straight back and Caleb had heard the approaching horses just about the same time the ferry touched the bank. A quick glance told Caleb straightaway that two of the riders were Sven Olfsen and Clem Gordon.

He almost made the small ferry capsize as he forced his horse to leap on to it, yelling at the ferryman to cast off and get the hell out of it.

'There's other folk wantin' to cross!' objected the man. 'I'd better wait for 'em.'

Caleb drew a gun and held it at the man. 'I said get this heap of wood on its way. If you don't, I reckon I can, an' you might just be feedin' the fishes. Now move it!'

The man chose not to question the preacher any further. They were about ten yards out from the bank when the four riders finally reached them, but Sven knew what to expect and had ordered the other three to dismount before the ferry. They took cover behind some rocks and started to shoot. Bullets thudded into the rotten timbers, but the current was rapidly taking the ferry beyond the range of ordinary hand guns. They did fire a couple of rounds with rifles, but the ferry was soon beyond accurate range of even these.

'Sorry about that, my friend,' said Caleb to the wide-eyed ferryman. 'Just a few grateful parishioners seeing me off.'

The man still looked wide-eyed and seemed unsure if Caleb was telling the truth or just joking. He finally decided that he must be joking.

'Do you allus have that effect on your congregations? I've been to church a couple of times an' I got to confess I found the sermons deadly borin', but I don't think anyone ever decided to try an' kill the preacher 'cos of it.'

'I dare say there have been a great many who felt like doing just that,' grinned Caleb. 'It's a long story and no concern of yours. How far is the fort from Benson?'

'Benson is the fort,' said the man, pushing against the steering rudder with all his might to bring the ferry head on to the bank. Caleb marvelled at the agility of the man, who was so thin it seemed that a good breath of wind would blow him away. 'There's quite a sizeable town grown up around the fort,' continued the ferryman. 'Even got its own sheriff these days, ever since the army refused to accept responsibility for civil matters.'

'Who's the commanding officer?' asked Caleb.

'Colonel Oliver...don't know his given name, he's just known as "Colonel". They do say all he's doin' is seein' his time out 'til he retires.'

'Colonel Oliver,' repeated Caleb. 'The sign said Benson was another fifteen miles. That about right?'

'If that's what the sign says, then I reckon that's how far it is,' agreed the man. 'Personally, I don't know how far a mile is, ain't never had the need to know, so I never bothered.' He looked back across the river at the four men staring at them. 'Unless you learned how to fly, Reverend, I'd say you ain't never gonna make it to Benson, nor no other place 'ceptin' maybe heaven or hell.'

'I can't go to either of those places,' smiled Caleb. 'I haven't booked my place yet.'

The ferry bumped against the bank and Caleb glanced at his watch. It had taken them about eight minutes to cross, but even allowing for the return journey, sixteen minutes was not enough to keep him clear of them.

His horse was older and nowhere near as fast as theirs appeared to be and he did not really fancy the idea of having to face the four of them in a shoot out—if it should come to that. It was far more likely that a straight fight was out of the question; he would be surrounded and probably shot in the back. He glanced up at the ropes which stretched across the river, along which a pulley ran to hold the boat.

'Fifty cents!' said the ferryman, holding out his hand.

'How would you like to make that fifty dollars?' grinned Caleb.

The man licked his lips and glanced back across the river and then sadly shook his head.

'My life's worth more'n fifty dollars,' he muttered.

'I take your point,' admitted Caleb.

'However, I am quite sure there must be ways to delay bringing them over. Supposing that rope was to break?'

'It did once,' said the man. 'Took three days to get the ferry goin' again.'

'Three days?' smiled Caleb. 'That should do just fine.'

'You'd have to cut the rope yourself Make it look like I wasn't agreein'. Only trouble is, this crossin' is so important, the army's made a law which says that anyone deliberately cuttin' the rope gets shot.'

'A bit drastic!' said Caleb. 'OK, so we can't cut rope. I'm sure you can stall them somehow.'

'Fifty dollars?' queried the man.

'Fifty dollars!' confirmed Caleb.

'For that kinda money, I reckon it can be arranged,' the man grinned. 'How long you reckon you need? Sometimes the pulley gets snagged halfway across, usually when the boat's empty. Don't know why that should be.'

'I could do with an hour at the very least,' said Caleb. 'Once I'm in Benson, I doubt they would have the nerve to kill me, not with so many witnesses, especially the army.'

'Sometimes I can free the snag in about five minutes,' said the man. 'Sometimes it can take half an hour or more. It's 'cos the rope comes off the pulley an' jams.'

'Just make certain that it takes an hour,' said Caleb.

'Tell you what, Preacher,' laughed the man, 'it'd look a whole lot better if'n you was to hit me or somethin'. Make it look like you was tryin' to delay things. I could lie doggo for a while an' then, when I start back across, the rope can jam up.'

'Hit you?' queried Caleb, looking at the frail body of the ferryman. 'I reckon even one tap would break your jaw.'

'You don't have to do it for real!' objected the man. 'They can't see what's really happenin' from over there. Just pretend.'

Caleb grinned. 'You got it! First though, here's your fifty...'

He slipped the note to the man. 'Now here comes the punch...'

He swung his fist and let the punch

ride past the fragile jaw, but the ferryman played his part well and thudded into the bottom of the boat, from where he grinned up at Caleb.

'Best of luck, Preacher!' he said.

Caleb led his horse off the ferry, mounted and looked across the river. He waved briefly at the men, laughed loudly, which he was certain could be heard across the river and then spurred his horse forward.

The ride out of the canyon and the ferry was almost the same as the other side. It took him a little over fifteen minutes to reach the top, where he turned and looked down.

The ferryman was still lying in the bottom of the boat and the four men were still waiting patiently on the other side, although they had been joined by another rider. The ferryman appeared to have seen Caleb and took it as his cue to get up and start back across the river. Caleb did not wait to see what happened next.

It took almost two and a half hours for Caleb to reach Benson, longer than he had expected, but then he had not really pushed his horse. How far behind the others were, he had no idea, but there was no sign of them as he entered the town.

He looked at his pocket watch, saw that it was just after five o'clock and wondered if he would manage to see Colonel Oliver that evening. Having experienced army discipline and routine, he had serious doubts. However, he had to try.

'I'd like to see Colonel Oliver,' he announced to the guard at the gate of Fort Benson which was, as the ferryman had said, in the centre of town.

'Colonel Oliver ain't seein' nobody!' grunted the guard, not sure how to treat Caleb. Had he been a white preacher or only a normal black man, there would have been no problem, but a black preacher was something he had never come across before.

'Why not?' asked Caleb.

'Ain't none of your business why not!' grumbled the guard. He turned and called out in the direction of the guardroom. 'Sergeant! There's a ni...black preacher here what wants to see the colonel.'

The sergeant emerged from the guard-house and shambled across to Caleb, where he eyed him up and down with a cynical smile on his face. 'Long way from home, ain't you?' he said.

'Home is where I make it,' replied Caleb. 'I have business I would like to discuss with Colonel Oliver.'

Again the sergeant's eyes ran up and down Caleb. 'Business! Can't see what possible business either a black or a preacher could have with the colonel.'

'I suggest that he be left to decide that,' sighed Caleb.

'Mister Preacher!' grated the sergeant. 'One reason there's a guard on the fort is to keep out folk who don't have no right bein' inside. Another reason is to make sure that our officers don't have every stranger with what they call business, pesterin' them when it ain't necessary. Anyhow, what is this business you've got to discuss?'

'I think that's better left for ears other than yours,' said Caleb.

The sergeant appeared unruffled at this apparent slight against him. He simply shrugged his shoulders and turned away. 'Suit yourself, it sure don't matter none to me. Anyhow, you can't see the colonel, he's away an' ain't due back until late tonight.'

Caleb realized that he was getting nowhere and decided to leave the matter alone for the time being. He doffed his hat to the guard and rode away from the fort.

The first hotel he came to claimed to be fully booked, although Caleb had doubts about the truth of that, but he chose not to argue; there was no shortage of hotels in Benson. The second hotel did appear to be fully booked, it had a sign in the window proclaiming the fact. At the third hotel, the clerk flatly refused to give him a room, simply because he was black.

'It don't matter none if you're a preacher or not,' said the man. 'I don't allow blacks or Indians in my hotel.'

'At least you're honest about it,' smiled Caleb. 'I could go on all evening looking for a room. Perhaps you wouldn't mind telling me where I would be welcome.'

'Ain't nowhere you'd be exactly welcome,' grinned the clerk, 'but Bennet's Hotel, just around the corner, don't usually mind too much. I've known 'em take blacks before now. Good job you're black an' not an Indian. There ain't nowhere would take Indians, not even the doss house an' they'll take almost everybody. Maybe you could try there. Twenty cents a night is all it costs, but that don't include no meals.'

'I can afford the best,' said Caleb.

'I wouldn't go shoutin' that too loud either,' smiled the clerk. Actually, Caleb quite liked the man, despite his proclaimed bias against blacks. 'This may be an army town, but that don't make it any safer than anywheres else. In fact, I reckon it makes it worse. The place is full of gamblers tryin' to take the wages off the soldiers as soon as they get it. If they don't get it, there's more'n enough whores who are only too willin'. No sir, it don't do to make it known you've got money on you an' that applies if you're white or black. Only thing is, folk is less likely to take notice if you're black.'

'I'll try this Bennet's Hotel,' said Caleb. 'I thank you for the warning although I normally think of things like that. I wonder, could you answer me another question?'

'You can always ask!' grinned the clerk.

'I have to get to see Colonel Oliver, but it would appear that the guards are very reluctant to let me see him. Is there anywhere I could get to meet him without having to go through layers of underlings first?'

'Nothin' easier!' grinned the clerk. 'The colonel loves to gamble an' he plays in the Wheel of Fortune—that's just down the street—every night without fail.'

'I'm told he's out of town.'

The clerk grinned broadly. 'Which means he's visitin' with the widow Armitage! Don't bother about that, he'll be in the Wheel just about eight o'clock as usual.'

'He must be either a very lucky gambler or be fortunate enough to be able to afford to lose,' said Caleb.

'Let's just say he don't very often lose,' laughed the clerk. 'I reckon the Wheel let him win sometimes just 'cos he's a good advertisement for them. It's a sure fact it's the busiest gamin' joint in town since he started goin' in there.'

An elderly, well-dressed man came into the lobby of the hotel and scowled at Caleb and the clerk, making plain his disapproval. Caleb decided not to embarrass the clerk further.

'I thank you for your help!' he said, making sure the elderly man heard. 'Bennet's Hotel, you said...'

The clerk nodded. 'Once again, thank you.' He turned and grinned broadly at the elderly man, raised his hat and said, 'Greetings, brother!' He knew full well that the man would take great exception to being called 'brother', but he could not resist the temptation to goad.

The man simply stood and stared, open-mouthed, but as soon as Caleb had left, he was ranting at the clerk for even allowing a black man as far as the lobby.

SIX

The clerk at Bennet's Hotel was very surly and most unhelpful, but he did not refuse Caleb a room, although he did insist on payment in advance of two dollars a night, which included breakfast. Caleb paid for one night, since he was not sure just how long his business would take.

The hotel was clean and comfortable and although the bedroom he was allocated was small and at the back of the building, it was clean and plenty big enough for his use. He found out later that he had not been put at the back because of his colour, but because he had just managed to secure the only room left in the hotel.

Even though his room was at the back, he had a good view out over the street and, as he stood idly staring, he saw four riders pass by, two of whom he recognized, Sven Olfsen and Clem Gordon, who had his arm in a sling. He had vague recollections of seeing the other two in Reno, but that was all.

His horse had been stabled in the hotel's own stables, just below his room so he could not follow the men easily, but he decided to see where they went.

They were almost out of sight at the far end of the street, when he emerged from the hotel, but caught a glimpse of them as they rounded the corner at the bottom. Making no attempt to hide, he hurried down the street but when he reached the corner, there was no sign of them. The street appeared to be made up almost entirely of small warehouses, but there was a large building at the far end, which was about as far as the street seemed to go.

'What's that place?' he asked a man passing by.

'Doss house!' grunted the man, with obvious disgust. Caleb could not be sure if the disgust was aimed at him or at the doss house. At least he was now reasonably sure where the four men were staying. This seemed confirmed when one of them came out and led their horses across the street to another building. Caleb had not seen the horses in the alley at the side.

Having fixed in his mind the faces of the other two men, Caleb decided it was time he had something to eat. He could have eaten at his hotel, but he wanted to see more of what the town was like. He found an eating place easily enough and the rather large lady served up a very good meal. She seemed quite proud of the fact that a preacher had chosen her place to eat.

'We've got three preachers in town,' she said, 'but none of 'em have ever been in here; don't know why. Father McGuire keeps sayin' he'll come, but he ain't never been yet.'

'Three preachers!' said Caleb, rather surprised.

'Sure,' said the woman. 'Father McGuire is a Catholic priest, I ain't sure what the others are. I'm Catholic myself too. You thinkin' of settin' up here too?'

'I don't think so,' grinned Caleb. 'The Lord would seem well served here.'

'Ain't no black preacher though,' smiled the woman. 'We've got a few blacks livin' here. I reckon they'd appreciate a black preacher.'

'Perhaps they would,' smiled Caleb, 'but not this particular black preacher. That was an excellent meal, I thank you.' He handed the fifty cents for the cost of the meal and wandered out on to the street. He had located the Wheel of Fortune before he had found the eating house and he decided to go back to it.

It was now almost seven o'clock, but the Wheel of Fortune, although open for business, was completely empty. A bartender nodded to him and told him the action never got going until about eight, but he was welcome to drink if he wanted one. Caleb decided to take up the offer.

'I understand Colonel Oliver comes in here every night,' he said casually as he sipped a glass of good beer.

'Every night 'ceptin Sunday,' confirmed the bartender. 'You know him?'

'Never met him in my life,' admitted

124

Caleb. 'I need to have a talk with him, but it seems the guards are either very protective or they just won't allow a black preacher anywhere near him.'

'They just don't like blacks,' grinned the bartender. 'Other folk have tried to get to see him in the fort, but they've almost always had to speak to him in here first. He won't talk business in here though, but if he thinks you've got somethin' interestin' to talk about, he'll arrange a meetin' at the fort.'

'That's all I ask,' said Caleb. 'What time does he get in?'

'You can set your watch by him,' replied the bartender. 'Eight-fifteen on the dot, even when he's been visitin' the widow Armitage.'

'That's the second time someone's mentioned her,' smiled Caleb. 'Ain't he married then?'

'I heard he lost his wife about five years ago. It ain't him who's runnin' after Mrs Armitage though, more like her who's chasin' after him. Her husband was a major, killed in a ridin' accident two years ago. Ever since then she's been after the colonel.'

'Plainly a woman who enjoys the security the army has to offer,' said Caleb. 'Eight-fifteen, you say? I think I'll just take a look around for an hour, I'll be back about eight. Perhaps you could point out the colonel when he comes in. I don't imagine he plays in his uniform.'

'He's done that before now,' laughed the bartender, 'but it ain't usual. Sure, be here an' I'll point him out.'

In the main street, Caleb saw his four pursuers staring glumly into a rather seedy looking eating house and it was very obvious that they could not afford even the twenty cents because he had looked in the same place himself earlier. Many might have felt that his next move was completely stupid, but Caleb thought he was safe enough. He crossed the street, unseen by any of them.

'Feelin' hungry, boys?' he laughed, coming up behind them.

They swung round and Sven Olfsen's immediate reaction was to go for his gun, but Adam Smith's hand clamped his and forced the gun back in its holster.

'Don't be so bloody stupid!' hissed Smith. Sven growled something which none of them understood and relaxed a little. 'I suppose you think you're safe,' sneered Smith. 'For the moment, I guess you are. You can't stay in this town for ever though.'

'I've been in worse places,' smiled Caleb. 'I saw you ride in earlier. What took you so long?'

'Bloody stupid ferry!' grumbled Clem Gordon. 'Damned thing got stuck halfway across, both ways. It took more'n twenty minutes each time to free it. That on top of you layin' out the ferryman for the same time gave you over an hour's start on us so we didn't try to catch up with you. We knew we'd find you here.'

'How did you know I'd come this way?' asked Caleb. 'I took the right-hand trail after leavin' that tradin' post.'

'Yeh, that had us fooled for a while,' admitted Jake Evans, 'but we guessed you must've cut across, so we did the same. We almost had you at that ferry though.'

'It was perhaps as well you didn't get there earlier,' smiled Caleb. 'If you had, it could be that you would all be fish food by now.'

They all scowled and said nothing, but Clem Gordon's glance through the dingy window of the eating house, just as a customer was being served with what looked like stew of some sort, followed by the licking of his lips made Caleb laugh and put his hand in his pocket to draw out a silver dollar.

'I guess you didn't come prepared for a long ride,' he said. 'The Good Lord said, "love thine enemies". Can't say as I can muster up much love for any of you, but I do hate to see a man starving. Here's a dollar; it'll cost you twenty cents apiece for the food. You can fight over the other twenty cents.'

'Stick your money up your arse!' grated Sven Olfsen.

The others looked in alarm at their leader and Adam Smith moved quickly, snatching the money from between Caleb's fingers.

'Pay no heed to him!' he snarled. 'Although I gotta admit I feel inclined to tell you the same, but I ain't so proud, money is money no matter where it comes from.'

'You comin', Sven?' said Clem as they headed for the door. Sven grumbled, snarled at Caleb but followed them inside. Caleb waved and smiled broadly at them through the dirty window. They scowled back and Sven made a couple of obscene gestures. Caleb laughed and left them alone. He later discovered that they could not afford even the twenty cents a night for the doss house and had had to sleep rough in some disused stables opposite.

He discovered the sheriff's office down a small street almost opposite the main gate to the fort and was tempted to tell the sheriff that four men seemed intent on killing him, but he decided against it, knowing full well that either he would not be interested or he would claim he could do nothing until they tried.

Further down the street, he met a group of black people, three men and two women. They seemed very surprised to see a black preacher and smiled weakly, but they made no attempt at conversation with him. By the time he returned to the Wheel of Fortune, Caleb had more or less seen all there was to see in Benson.

Soldiers were in evidence wherever he went and it was plain that the town survived courtesy of the army. He had seen towns like Benson before and he had also seen what happened to such places when the army moved out. With little evidence of anything else to sustain it, if the army did leave, Benson would simply die.

There were about a dozen customers in The Wheel of Fortune as he entered and all eyed him a little suspiciously, but whether this was because of the colour of his skin, his preacher's garb or the fact that he wore two guns, he could not be sure but, then again, whatever the reason, he was not bothered.

130

He called for a beer and the bartender told him that it was not quite time for the colonel although, according to Caleb's watch, it was a few minutes past his time. There was a large clock on a wall which indicated a time some seven minutes behind Caleb's.

Promptly, at eight-fifteen—according to the clock on the wall at least—a tall, military figure, dressed in a neat grey suit, entered. Caleb needed no telling that this was Colonel Oliver, although the bartender nudged him and nodded.

The colonel ordered a beer and a whisky and wandered across to a card table where, as yet, he was the only customer. Caleb picked up his beer and followed.

If the colonel was surprised to see a black man standing at his side, he did not show it. Eventually he turned and looked Caleb up and down and smiled slightly.

'First time I ever seen a preacher wearing guns!' he grinned. 'It isn't often any man wears two guns. Can you use them?'

'There's been more than one who's

131

found out I can,' replied Caleb. 'Colonel Oliver?'

'That's me,' nodded the colonel. 'Colonel Benjamin Oliver, Corps of Engineers. What can I do for you, Padre?'

'You could arrange to let your guards allow me into the fort,' smiled Caleb.

'We've got no need for a padre,' said the colonel. 'What business have you got in there?'

'Business that could be for your ears only,' said Caleb. 'I think you would find what I have to say very interesting.'

'If you're thinking of converting me to some crackpot idea, then you're wasting your time,' laughed the colonel. 'I've probably got my ticket booked for hell already.'

'I may be a preacher,' said Caleb, 'but that don't mean I have to talk, eat and sleep religion. Even us clerics do have other interests and it's surprising what information we pick up.'

Once again the colonel looked Caleb up and down and smiled. 'With two guns, which you reckon you can use, the image of a preacher doesn't sit too easy on you. From your bearing too, I'd say you've seen military service.'

'Third US Cavalry,' grinned Caleb. 'Lieutenant Caleb Black at your service, sir!'

'Lieutenant!' nodded the colonel. 'Yeh, I heard there were a few black officers. What made you give it up, you probably had a good career ahead of you?'

'Black officers were only allowed to command black soldiers,' said Caleb. 'As for a career, I might have made major if I'd been very lucky, probably no more than captain though. Besides, I felt this need to serve God.'

'Funny way to serve God, 'laughed the Colonel. 'I've heard about fightin' the good fight, but I didn't realize He was recruitin' real gunfighters. Caleb Black, eh, black by colour and Black by name. Looking at you, I'd say you could be pretty black by nature too. OK, so you've got something you want to talk to me about, well I'm here, start talkin'.'

Three other men were heading towards

the table, which rather pleased Caleb since he did not really feel inclined to talk in the saloon.

'You'll probably need to consult your records,' said Caleb. 'Just for the moment I'll just say that it concerns a shipment of gold that apparently went missing, probably from the Fifth Cavalry, but I can't be too sure of that.'

Colonel Oliver laughed. 'That old one! Sure, I know about that gold, so does almost everybody in the army and everywhere else I dare say. There's a reward of fifty thousand dollars out on it. I don't suppose that could be influencing you in any way?'

'I didn't know about the reward,' said Caleb, 'and that's the truth. All I know is I've a pretty good idea where it might be found.'

Colonel Oliver looked up at Caleb and could see that he was in deadly earnest. The cynical smile vanished from his face and he nodded. 'You're right, Padre, this isn't the place to talk. Be at the fort at eight in the morning. The guards will have instructions to let you in and escort you to my office. I'd better warn you though, I reckon I've heard every tale in the book when it comes to that gold. The only thing that makes it interesting is that so far, there's been no trace of it and it's been missing a long time now.'

'I'll be there,' promised Caleb, 'and I can assure you that I do believe I know where it is. I am not in the habit of wasting my time or anyone else's, besides which, there are four men in town who have been sent to kill me simply because of what I know.'

The colonel looked up sharply as the other three men shuffled into their chairs around the table. 'Sheriff's the man for things like that,' he said.

'Since they haven't, as yet, done anything, I don't suppose the sheriff would be all that interested and if I'm dead, I don't suppose I'd be all that interested.'

'Eight in the mornin',' grunted the colonel. 'Now, as a preacher, I don't suppose you approve of gambling, but

I'm afraid it's my one vice.'

'That and the widow Armitage,' grinned Caleb.

'You have been busy!' smiled the colonel.

In actual fact, although he officially preached against gambling and the demon drink, Caleb was quite partial to both, although on a very limited basis. He decided to join in a few hands of blackjack for no other reason than he had nothing else to do.

He stayed at the table for twenty hands of which he won fourteen, leaving himself with a quite handsome profit of more than $200. The dealer seemed quite relieved when Caleb finally picked up his winnings and left the Wheel of Fortune.

On his exploration of Benson, Caleb had come across an orphanage tucked well out of sight in the poorer end of the town. It appeared to be run by nuns and, although not of that faith, he had always greatly admired their dedication and cheerfulness. He had already decided what he was going to do with the $200.

A middle-aged nun answered his knock on the door and was rather surprised at his garb. At first she seemed unsure if she ought to let him in or not, but another, obviously more senior nun, came up behind her, smiled broadly at Caleb and allowed him to enter.

'Welcome to St Margaret's Orphanage,' greeted the senior nun. 'I'm Sister Claire and this is Sister Mary. You must forgive her for seeming to be so unwelcoming, but we do get some very funny men here from time to time, mostly trying to buy children, usually girls.'

'Buy the children?' queried Caleb, as he was ushered into a small room, devoid of all furniture except for two chairs opposite each other. The woodwork was very highly polished and the floor so slippery it was almost lethal.

'Oh, yes,' said the nun, seriously, 'it's not at all uncommon.'

'And do you sell them?'

'Oh dear, no,' assured the nun.

They were interrupted as the door opened and another, much younger nun peered round. 'A word with you, Sister, if it is convenient.'

'Is it important?' asked the senior nun.

'I do believe it is,' replied the young nun.

Sister Claire sighed, apologized to her visitor and left him alone in the room. He could hear hushed voices in the passage, but was unable to make out what was said. When she returned, Sister Claire gave him a slightly awkward look, but said nothing about what the urgent business had been.

'Now, what were we talking about?' asked Sister Claire. 'Oh, yes, the buying and selling of the children. Well, we are an orphanage and we have a duty to care for unwanted children. Usually they are left here by single girls who have got themselves into trouble with one of the soldiers. Of course, we do try to place them with families who wish to adopt, but I am afraid that we do not have the means to check everyone who claims they want to. Briefly, there are times when our children end up working as little more than slaves...' She blushed slightly at using the word and glanced at the floor. 'Sometimes the girls are destined for some brothel or other.'

'It's all right,' laughed Caleb. 'Neither of my parents were slaves, they were freemen from Boston, my father was a seaman.'

Sister Claire blushed again. 'I...it...sometimes we have men calling here offering to buy the children. It seems that even boys have some use in a brothel, although I can't think what.'

Caleb decided that he would not enlighten her. 'It must be quite expensive, keeping a child fed and clothed.'

'Very!' said Sister Claire, almost able to smell the money in Caleb's pocket. 'Sometimes the men offer us as much as a hundred dollars for a girl. It seems that young, virgin girls are highly prized in that very seedy world.'

'And you have never sold any child on that basis?'

'Of course not!' Sister Claire sat up indignantly.

'I meant no offence, Sister,' apologized Caleb.

'None taken!' she assured. 'Anyhow, we keep the children until they are fourteen if we can't find places for them.' She sighed deeply and looked sad. 'Unfortunately we just can't afford to keep them beyond that age and it is all too often the case that the girls end up in the brothels anyway. The boys seem to find work, a good many even join the army since there is little else. We are also in imminent danger of being closed down.'

'Closed down!' said Caleb. 'Why's that?'

'Unfortunately we do not own this property. It was given to us by a man who had made a fortune from supplying the army. However, he has died and his son is intent on foreclosing on us. He's given us the chance to raise the money to buy the place but it is very expensive, he wants forty thousand dollars!'

'Forty thousand!' exclaimed Caleb. 'No property is worth that much!'

'I thought that too,' said the nun, 'but that's the price he wants. It is a very solid building, just about the only place, apart from the jail and the fort, that's built of brick. It is very large as well, don't be deceived by the front, it goes back a long way and there is a large paddock as well.'

'Even so, forty thousand!' muttered Caleb, beginning to feel that his intended offering of $200 was almost insulting.

'The army have offered thirty-five thousand,' said Sister Claire. 'So, since the banks only say how sorry they are and it would be a pity all our good work was lost, they suddenly become very deaf when I mention a loan. Mind you, the truth of it is that even if we did get a loan, we could never afford to repay it.'

'What will you do?'

'We don't know, we haven't decided yet, but I expect we shall have to move away from Benson. We can always restart somewhere else I suppose. We have another month to raise the money or get out.'

'I'm sure the Good Lord will provide,' said Caleb, not at all convinced by his own platitudes.

'We can but pray!' agreed Sister Claire. 'Now, Father...'

'I'm not a "Father",' interrupted Caleb. 'I'm just an ordinary preacher. The name is Caleb Black...'

'Black by colour...'

'Black by name!' grunted Caleb. 'If I had a dollar for every time that's been said to me, I'd be a very rich man by now.'

'I'm sorry,' demurred Sister Claire, 'I should have realized. Well now, Preacher Black, I'm quite certain you didn't come here just to listen to all our troubles. What can I do for you?'

'More what I can do for you,' smiled Caleb. 'Although, after finding out your problems, I'm not sure it will be much help.' He handed her the $200 he had won at the gambling table. 'You could say this is a contribution from the Wheel of Fortune at the other end of town.' She looked at him quizzically. 'I must confess to having succumbed to the doubtful pleasures of the gaming table and I was fortunate enough to win this money. Since I have no need for it, I wondered if it might help you.'

Sister Claire smiled broadly. 'It was the Lord's way of helping. There must be at least two hundred dollars here and it is more than welcome. You would be surprised at how little we do have to exist on at times. I thank you from the bottom of my heart.'

'I only wish I could do more,' apologized Caleb. 'Can't your local priest, Father McGuire I think he's called, do anything?'

Sister Claire smiled indulgently. 'He has his job to do, we have ours. I think he secretly disapproves of our work.'

Caleb nodded his head. He had come across priests and other clergy like that before. 'Well, Sister, I have done what I came to do and now I must bid you goodbye.' He smiled at her. 'It could just be that you may not have to move. The Lord does indeed work in mysterious ways.'

'We can but hope and pray,' smiled the nun. 'Now, I must leave you to let yourself out, if you don't mind.'

Caleb smiled, replaced his hat and left the orphanage. He had not reached the corner of the building when he was suddenly confronted by four dark figures, one with his arm in a sling.

'Been to make your peace have you?' sneered Adam Smith. 'Maybe it's as well; your time's up, Preacher!'

He should have expected something like this, but somehow he had not. There was no chance of going for his guns, so he simply stood and waited for the inevitable.

'It could just be that your time is up as well!' came a female voice from behind them.

Sister Claire stepped out of the alley at the side of the orphanage, a rifle held steady at her waist and she gave the distinct impression that she knew how to use it and was not afraid to. She motioned with the rifle for the men to move. Only Sven Olfsen had drawn his gun and he seemed torn between shooting Caleb and the nun. In the end he decided that neither was a good idea.

'Take their guns, Reverend,' instructed the nun. 'Men like them shouldn't be allowed to carry guns, they could easily kill someone.'

'Keep out of this, Sister!' snarled Adam Smith. 'We've come to do a job an' we intend doin' it.'

'On your way!' she ordered, seeing that Caleb had taken their guns. 'In these parts even nuns have been known to shoot folk.'

The men looked at each other, then at the nun and finally at Caleb, whom they chose to sneer at and mutter something about hiding behind a woman's skirts. However, they quickly left the scene.

'I thank you,' grinned Caleb. 'How did you know they were there?'

'That's what Sister Emmanuel had to tell me,' explained Sister Claire. 'She was in the alley and overheard them talking as they waited for you. I don't know what you've done to deserve being killed, but I'm very glad I was able to prevent it.'

'Not half as glad as I am!' laughed Caleb.

'You are quite right,' said the nun, 'the Lord does move in mysterious ways!'

SEVEN

Sister Claire had taken charge of the guns, saying that the men could collect them when Caleb left town. It was a situation Caleb was quite happy with and he had the feeling that the Sisters of St Margaret were more than capable of looking after themselves.

Rather curious as to why such a price of $40,000 should be asked for the orphanage, Caleb idly wandered down the alley at the side and was very surprised at the actual size of the building. Sister Claire had said that it was a lot bigger than it looked from the front and this was indeed the case. It stretched back almost fifty yards, one of the largest buildings he had seen since leaving Boston and beyond that was what Sister Claire had called a paddock, in reality what looked like a five or six acre field. Even so, the price seemed extortionately high.

It seemed to have three floors and quite a considerable number of outbuildings.

'So the army are interested in it too,' he mused. 'What would they want it for, barracks maybe?'

However, as much as he sympathized with the problems facing the sisters, there was nothing he could do about it and it certainly was not his problem, but he intended to ask Colonel Oliver what the army's interest was.

He had expected to meet Sven Olfsen and his cronies again, but in the now bustling streets of Benson, there was no sign of them and, knowing that they had no money, he assumed they had simply gone to ground. He wandered about for the best part of another hour, resisting the temptation to try his luck at the blackjack table once again, before returning to his hotel for the night.

Ever wary, he slept with one ear on the alert that night, although there was no trouble. It could have been that the men did not know where he was staying or that they had decided to wait. He fancied that they were simply biding their time.

Eight o'clock the following morning found Caleb being escorted from the main gate of the fort to the office of Colonel Oliver. This time the colonel was in uniform and looked quite different from the previous night in the Wheel of Fortune. The colonel indicated a chair opposite his desk, dismissed the escort and settled down in a huge, leather chair behind the desk, clasped his hands across his chest, leaned back and smiled at Caleb, waiting for the preacher to speak.

'I trust you had a profitable evening,' said Caleb, by the way of breaking the ice. 'I did, but then I lost it a lot quicker than I had won it.'

'Yeh,' smiled the colonel, 'I noticed you left with somethin' like two hundred. How come you lost it?'

'Well, I don't suppose I can truthfully say I lost it, I didn't gamble it away or have it stolen, I gave it to Sister Claire at the orphanage.'

'A good cause,' agreed Colonel Oliver.

'Yes, I showed a profit, not as much as you, but quite healthy, although I have better use for it than giving it to the orphans.'

'Speaking of the orphanage,' said Caleb. 'Sister Claire tells me that the army is interested in buying the place. She tells me that she has to raise forty thousand dollars or get out. I can see that it is a huge place and no doubt just about the most valuable property, apart from the fort, in town, but what would the army want with it? Surely you have enough already?'

'It's no secret,' smiled the colonel. 'The government intends to extend the base, make it into an engineer training fort. That means we're goin' to need a whole lot more accommodation and the orphanage would be ideal. As to the price, I know it sounds a lot, and it is, but in these parts even a rickety wooden shack can fetch ten times what it does anywhere else.'

'Personally, I wouldn't have thought it was all that suitable for you,' said Caleb. 'For a start, it isn't exactly in the best part of town and it is a fair way from the fort.'

'I don't think it's really the place,' agreed the colonel, 'but I'm only actin' on orders. I don't think the generals really want it either, not permanently that is. There are plans to extend the fort, we've got the space, but it would solve a problem in the short term.'

'And create a long-term problem for the orphans!' suggested Caleb. 'Still, it's none of my business, I was just curious.'

'And the orphans are not the problem of the army,' said Colonel Oliver. 'Now, I'm a busy man, I haven't got the time to sit around socializing with anyone, including a preacher. You said you knew something about that gold. OK, let's hear it.'

'I was in a town called Reno before I came here,' said Caleb. 'You may well know of it...' The colonel nodded. 'Well, in that town, there is a man, a coloured man, like me, whose job it is to clean out cesspits...'

'Aaron Williams,' interrupted the colonel, glancing at a piece of paper attached to a file on his desk. 'I know exactly what you are goin' to say, Reverend. This Aaron

Williams claims he found some gold bars at the bottom of one of these pits he was cleaning out. We've already investigated that claim, but we didn't find a damned thing. There were thirty gold bars in that shipment and they've all disappeared. We know the markings and if we could just find one would be a start. You're not telling me anything we didn't already know, Mr Black.'

'They may have been melted down by now,' Caleb pointed out.

'Maybe so,' agreed the colonel, 'but that amount of gold comin' on to the market would have been noticed very quickly. No, we think the gold is probably still in bars and hidden somewhere with perhaps the occasional bar being melted so as not to create suspicion.'

'So you didn't believe Aaron Williams?'

Colonel Oliver smiled and opened the file. 'It was not a case of not believing him,' he said. 'But at the time there was a hell of a lot of publicity and you wouldn't believe the number of cranks and weirdos who claimed to know where it was. Mind you, at the time there was no reason to think that this Williams was anything but on the level, but later we heard that he was probably just trying to get a retired cavalry officer into trouble. It seems they don't get on with each other.'

'Colonel George Baker,' smiled Caleb. 'We've met, just the once, which is rather strange.'

Colonel Oliver looked quizzically at the preacher for a moment. 'Can't see nothin' strange about that. You didn't live in Reno, did you?'

'Perhaps I'd better explain something,' smiled Caleb. He took a small, hardbacked book out of his pocket and handed it to Colonel Oliver. 'I told you that I was once a lieutenant in the Third Cavalry. That is my certificate of service and discharge papers to prove my claim.'

The colonel examined the document, smiled and handed it back to Caleb. 'That looks all in order, Lieutenant. You didn't have to prove a thing to me, I believed you the first time.'

'The point is,' said Caleb. 'I wanted to

add weight to what I have to say. I was in command of a black detachment of the Third Cavalry, but for a time, two months in fact, I was sent to the Fifth Cavalry to investigate the possibility of introducing a wholly black detachment with them. Now, at the time, the commanding officer of the Fifth Cavalry was one Colonel George Baker. My duties brought me into regular contact with him...'

Colonel Benjamin Oliver leaned forward slightly and smiled at Caleb knowingly. 'And you're about to claim that this Colonel George Baker and the Colonel George Baker who lives in Reno and claims to be the real one, are not one and the same man!'

'You don't seem too surprised,' said Caleb.

'I ought to be, but I'm not,' admitted Oliver. 'I met the man once when I went to Reno and there was something about him that just didn't ring true. Oh, the signature was the same and he knew everything he was supposed to know, but there was just that something. I even thought about following it up, but I never got round to it. I thought I was just being stupid.'

'I can assure you,' smiled Caleb, 'that the Colonel George Baker in Reno is not the real colonel.'

'Well now, that is interesting!' grinned Colonel Oliver, sitting back and clasping his hands across his chest again. 'That could explain quite a few things. However, we gave that area a thorough goin' over when we looked for the gold and, as far as the army is concerned, there is nothing there, certainly nothing that would make my superiors think again.'

'Not even if it can be proven that it is not Colonel Baker?'

'All we could do would be to prosecute the man for illegally drawing an army pension. As far as I know there's no law which says a man can't give himself whatever title he wants.'

'I know that, Colonel,' said Caleb. 'The thing is, who is the man in Reno who claims to be Colonel Baker? If you knew that, it could give you a lead as to where the gold is, or at least what happened to it.'

Colonel Oliver consulted the papers in the file for a time before he spoke. 'It looks like the man in Reno is drawing an army pension,' he said. 'Even so, it's very much your word against his, unless we can come up with someone else who knew the real colonel. That shouldn't be too difficult though.' He thumbed his way through several other papers before suddenly stopping and examining one a little more closely.

He smiled and looked up at the preacher, whistling slightly. He drew the particular document from the file and held it for Caleb to examine.

'It would help if I knew what I was supposed to be looking for,' said Caleb, studying the document closely.

'Names, man!' grinned Colonel Oliver. 'Look at the names!'

This time it was Caleb's turn to whistle slightly as he read the document again. 'Eli Carter...'

'And Eli Carter is the man who runs

most of Reno,' said the colonel. 'Not only that, look at the name at the bottom.'

'G. Baker!' read Caleb. 'G. Baker, Quartermaster Corporal!'

'G. Baker,' smiled the colonel. 'I'll almost guarantee that the "G" stands for George. I'll have it checked out straight away and, unless there are also two men with the name of Eli Carter, horse dealer, I'll guarantee it's the same man as Eli Carter in Reno.'

'As a quartermaster corporal, it is quite possible, indeed almost certain, that he would have access to the gold,' said Caleb. 'Not only that, he would have been in an ideal position to see the real colonel's signature and to forge it.'

Colonel Oliver nodded and leaned back again. 'I can't see how we didn't notice that before,' he said. 'Mind you, it now raises the question as to what happened to Colonel George Baker. It sure looks like the man in Reno is drawin' the army pension due to Colonel Baker, but what happened?'

'You must know that getting rid of a

body out in the desert or almost anywhere else is not all that difficult,' Caleb pointed out. 'Even if the bones are found later, there's no way they could be identified.'

'Sure, that's the easy part,' agreed the colonel. 'OK, Mr Preacher Black, I've got to admit that there's something in your story. The thing is, if you could come up with just one bar of gold which could be identified, my superiors would have no option but to go in search again and take action against the bogus colonel.'

'Can't you take action on your own?' suggested Caleb.

'I could, but if I didn't come up with the goods, my head would roll, nothin' more certain and, since I've only got another twelve months to go before I retire, I'm not all that anxious to cause too much trouble. Mind you, if I could recover the gold, or at least account for where it's gone, it'd sure be a big feather in my cap.'

'Just supposing I could come up with something?' said Caleb.

'You're a free man, which is more than I am,' smiled the colonel. 'I've got a master,

158

just as powerful as any slavemaster, it's called the army. You ought to know that. Weren't you ever told to salute it if it moved and paint it if it didn't?'

'Sure!' laughed Caleb. 'Which was one reason for me quitting. OK, Colonel, I suggest you tell your superiors what we know so far and I'll see if I can come up with anything in Reno. It would be a great help if I knew what the markings were on that shipment.'

Colonel Oliver looked at Caleb and smiled slightly. 'I can't do that, that's classified information, we need it to make sure someone doesn't try to fool us with some other gold.' He stood up and turned over a couple of sheets of paper in the file before going to the door. 'I think my second-in-command, Major Travers ought to be told of this. I'll go and fetch him, I should only be five minutes.' He smiled knowingly and left the office, closing the door behind him.

Caleb had been very quick to take the hint and almost before the door had closed, he was examining the page that had been turned over in the file and was soon jotting down numbers and signs on a pad that had been conveniently placed alongside. By the time the colonel returned with Major Travers, who turned out to have a broad Scots accent, Caleb was sitting and closely examining the weave of his black frock coat.

For the benefit of Major Travers, the whole story was repeated and he seemed very impressed. He agreed that the information was too sensitive for them to take action without permission.

The Reverend Caleb Black left Fort Benson with the distinct feeling that action would not be too long in coming and he knew that it also meant a journey back to Reno. However, there was the slight problem of Sven Olfsen and his three cronies.

Caleb was well aware that they knew he had been into the fort and, even if they did not know why, if the information were to get back to Reno before either he or the army did, there was every chance that both George Baker and the gold would disappear.

As he left the fort, Caleb saw the four a little further down the street. He deliberately walked past them and raised his hat, calling 'Greetings, brothers!'

Back in his hotel room, the thought suddenly struck him that he had a wad of Wanted posters and, for want of something to do for the moment, he idly thumbed through them. He had not really expected to find anything, but there it was, a poster with a $100 reward for one Adam Smith, alias Adam Gates, alias Grant Gates. Wanted for three counts of robbery. There were no posters relating to the other three.

'Pity, that,' he said to himself. 'It'll get Smith out of the way, but it still leaves the others. I'll go tell the sheriff I know where Smith is so's he can arrange the reward money.'

The four men were waiting on the opposite side of the street as he came out of the hotel and they followed him to the sheriff's office where, for some reason, they suddenly disappeared.

There was a young man lounging behind a desk who looked up and, on seeing a black man, was about to sneer and swagger when he noticed the preacher's clothing. This rather threw him and he sat up nervously. Caleb decided that this young man could not possibly be the sheriff.

'I'd like a word with the sheriff,' said Caleb, deliberately standing menacingly over the young man, which made him very nervous indeed since at that angle, Caleb's six foot six inch height and very broad frame was very intimidating.

'I...I...I'm Deputy Sinclair,' grunted the young man, somehow managing to summon up hidden courage. 'What can I do for you...er Reverend?'

Caleb smiled and even felt slightly sorry for him. 'Well, Deputy Sinclair,' he boomed in his best pulpit voice. 'I know of a man in your town who has a hundred dollar reward out on him. Do you want me to bring him in, or will you?'

'Me?' said Deputy Sinclair, looking most alarmed.

'Yes, you,' Caleb boomed again. 'After all, it is the job of sheriffs and deputy sheriffs to arrest men who are wanted, is it not?'

'I...I guess so,' faltered Deputy Sinclair.

'Then I put it to you that you are failing in your duty by allowing such men to remain free.'

'And I put it to you that you are in the business of saving people's souls!' another voice boomed behind Caleb.

Caleb turned to face a man almost as big as himself, wearing the badge of office of a sheriff.

'You must be Sheriff Jordan,' smiled Caleb, extending his hand, which was refused by the new arrival. 'Caleb Black—the Reverend Caleb Black, at your service.'

Caleb had gleaned the name of the sheriff from the fact that it was painted above the door.

'Reverend!' grunted the sheriff. 'So what's all this about?' He pushed past Caleb and Deputy Sinclair respectfully vacated the desk for his superior.

'There is a man, possibly four, at present

163

in your town who is wanted by the law,' repeated Caleb. 'His name is Adam Smith, alias Adam Gates, alias Grant Gates, apparently wanted for several robberies. The price on his head is one hundred dollars.'

'Peanuts!' grunted Jordan. 'For that kind of money it's hardly worth printin' the posters.' He sat down and lounged back in the chair and looked scornfully at the preacher. 'So what's your interest, Reverend? Concerned about the likely moral effect on society having a known criminal running loose?'

'On the contrary,' smiled Caleb. 'I am quite certain that society is more than capable of inflicting its own ills. No, my concern is rather more personal; this man, Adam Smith and his three companions are seemingly intent upon killing me. It is a matter of pure self-preservation which prompts me to request his arrest.'

Jordan laughed lightly. 'What the hell should anyone want to kill a preacher for? Maybe you preach a lousy sermon an' they think they're doin' society a favour in gettin' rid of you.' He looked more closely at the preacher and smiled again. 'First time I ever seen a preacher wearin' a gun. Are you sure you're a preacher?'

'Two guns!' corrected Caleb, pulling aside his coat to reveal the other one. 'And yes, I am a preacher and yes, I can use both guns very effectively.'

'And probably have done!' muttered Jordan. 'So, if you can use your guns, why the hell are you worried about bein' shot at by these men?'

'I am not normally in the business of killing,' said Caleb. 'As you say, my business is to save souls, not to condemn them. Now, I must ask you to arrest this man and possibly his companions. Although I do not normally refuse any rewards, in this instance you can donate it to the orphanage, their need is greater than mine.'

'Very noble of you!' grunted Jordan. 'OK, Reverend, I guess I have to agree with you that it's my duty to arrest wanted criminals and outlaws, although if I was to do that to every one of them who comes into town, it would be damned near empty sometimes. For the most part, unless they're real bad 'uns, I leave 'em alone providin' they don't force my hand. OK, where are they?'

'I believe they are bunking down in an old stable or barn opposite the doss house. They can't afford their prices. You needn't worry too much about them shooting at you, as far as I know they don't have any guns.'

'Don't have any guns!' laughed Jordan. 'Then just how the hell are they gonna kill you? They strike me as a mighty peculiar bunch of outlaws if they don't have guns!'

'You will find that Sister Claire at the orphanage has taken charge of their guns,' explained Caleb. 'It could be that they do have rifles though, I suppose.'

'Reverend!' sighed Jordan. 'I won't ask just how she came to have them, I might not believe the answer. You seem to know this man, Smith; how come?'

Caleb produced the Wanted poster and Jordan merely glanced at it. He opened a drawer and pulled out a large, thick file, in which there seemed to be hundreds of posters. He tossed the file to Caleb and then motioned Deputy Sinclair. Both men picked up their rifles and made for the door.

'While we're gone, you take a look through them. It could be that your other men are there. Since we're pickin' up one, we might as well make it worthwhile if we can.'

Before Caleb could reply, they had stomped out of the door. He smiled ruefully and proceeded to look through the Wanted posters.

He had looked through about half the file when he came across the posters of the three men he had killed in Reno and he pulled them out, intending to tell Sheriff Jordan, but the next three posters proved far more interesting. They were all of the other three men with Adam Smith.

It was about twenty minutes before the sound of scuffling and loud protests heralded the return of Sheriff Jordan and Deputy Sinclair as they herded four very angry men into the office. They saw Caleb and immediately made a lunge towards him, although a sharp prod from Deputy Sinclair's rifle prevented further action. Their language was not what a preacher should have heard, but Caleb simply smiled and said, 'Welcome, brothers!' This only succeeded in bringing forth a further torrent of abuse and threats. Deputy Sinclair herded the men through a door at the back of the office and the sound of a metal door could be heard slamming and being locked.

Caleb smiled and handed Jordan the three posters of Sven Olfsen—$200, Clem Gordon—$200 and Jake Evans—$100.

'That would seem to take care of that problem,' said Caleb. 'I thank you for your assistance, Sheriff—you too Deputy Sinclair. Your records are not quite up to date though, Sheriff...'

He handed Jordan the other three Wanted posters. 'These men are no longer wanted—they're dead.'

Jordan grunted and took the posters,

hardly giving them a glance. 'How'd you know that?'

'I killed them!' smiled Caleb.

Deputy Sinclair looked at the preacher and then at his superior with a look something akin to stupor and tried to say something, but the words ended in a meaningless babble.

'I think he's tryin' to say that preachers ain't usually in the business of killin'!' grinned Jordan. 'Don't worry about it, boy, I reckon this particular preacher ain't your usual run of preachers. I know I sure wouldn't like to get on the wrong side of his gun!' Both the sheriff and Caleb laughed. 'Now, Preacher Black, that makes a total of six hundred dollars reward. What do you want doin' with it?'

'Give it all to Sister Claire!' smiled Caleb. 'I must confess that I am rarely so generous, but there are exceptional circumstances. You had better collect those men's guns from her as well.'

'I must remember not to ask her what happened,' grinned Jordan. 'She's almost as crazy as you!'

EIGHT

'What the hell are you doin' back here?' demanded Sheriff McCauley as Caleb marched into his office. 'I had hoped that Reno had returned to somethin' like normal.'

'A little unfinished business,' replied Caleb, flopping into the chair opposite the sheriff's desk.

'Don't tell me, I'll lay odds it has somethin' to do with Colonel Baker.'

'Right first time!' grinned Caleb. 'But to give him his correct rank, he's Corporal George Baker, lately of the quartermaster's department of the Fifth Cavalry.'

'Corporal?' said McCauley, although he did not sound too surprised. 'You have been busy. Where'd you find that out?'

'Fort Benson,' replied Caleb. 'They've still got a file on the missing gold.'

'Don't know why folk can't just leave

that alone,' muttered McCauley. 'The army checked that one out ages ago.'

'And I reckon they're about to check it out again,' smiled Caleb. 'I just thought I'd better let you know what's goin' to happen, but both me and the army would be grateful if you didn't let on to anyone else.'

'Maybe I will, maybe I won't,' McCauley muttered again. 'What's in it for you if the gold is recovered?'

'Fifty thousand dollars,' said Caleb in a matter-of-fact way. 'That's the reward out for recovery.'

'And would fifty thousand take you well away from Reno?'

'A million miles!' grinned Caleb. 'That's a promise.'

'Just out of my territory would be enough,' said the sheriff. 'As long as you promised never to come back.'

'I think you can take that as fact,' agreed Caleb. 'Now, do you intend to warn anyone or not?'

McCauley looked hard at the preacher for quite a long time and eventually shook his head. 'I guess not, I reckon the army will be here whether or not, so the best thing I can hope for is that they find it pretty damned quick—or not, as the case may be—and get the hell out of it to leave us in peace. Have you got any idea where the gold might be?'

'Some,' lied Caleb. 'One thing is certain, at least by my book, it's still here somewhere. Oh, and don't be surprised if they arrest Baker. The charge will probably be drawing an army pension to which he is not entitled.'

'Mr Black!' sighed McCauley. 'As far as you're concerned, nothin' would surprise me any more. We haven't seen Sven Olfsen, Clem Gordon, Adam Smith or Jake Evans lately. Rumour has it that they were sent out after you. I don't suppose you know anythin' about where they might be now?'

'I know exactly where they are now!' grinned Caleb. 'They are at this very moment, in residence at the jail in Benson.'

'In jail?' The sheriff raised his eyebrows

slightly. 'How the hell did they end up in there?'

'It would appear that your records are not completely up to date,' said Caleb. 'I admit that you did have a Wanted poster out on Adam Smith, but you had nothing on the other three. Sheriff Jordan, at Benson, was more up to date than you, he had all four on his files, worth a total of six hundred. Not a lot, I agree, but it's enough to keep them out of circulation for a while.'

'You're makin' a steady income of outlaws,' muttered McCauley, 'that makes eighteen hundred. That's not bad at all, a damned sight more'n I can earn.'

'Twelve hundred,' corrected Caleb. 'I gave the other reward to a much needier cause than me.'

'It's your money!' sighed McCauley. 'OK, so just when is the army due here?'

'Sometime tomorrow, I believe,' replied Caleb. 'I told Colonel Oliver not to send a wire warning you; these things have a habit of suddenly becoming public knowledge.'

'I know what you mean,' nodded

McCauley. 'OK, I'll be ready for them when they do come. What's your next move?'

'Have a word with my friend Aaron,' said Caleb. 'I reckon that even by now, both Baker and Carter will know I'm back. I can only hope they don't take fright and run.'

'I don't reckon that's likely, not Eli Carter anyhow, everythin' he owns is here. Maybe Baker will, but I have my doubts, he's too old to run far.'

'I hope so,' said Caleb. 'Well, thank you, Sheriff, I'll go and see Aaron now.'

'He claimed he found some gold in a cesspit,' said McCauley. 'Nobody ever found nothin' though.'

'It's still around,' smiled Caleb. 'I'm certain of that.'

Aaron and Pearl Williams seemed over-joyed when Caleb knocked on the flimsy door of their shack and Pearl ushered him in, insisting that he take the best chair. Aaron was prepared to break open the whisky bottle again, but Caleb refused.

'What you back here for, Reveren'?'

asked Aaron. 'We didn't 'spect to see you again.'

'I need your help,' said Caleb. 'That gold you found once, have you any idea where it could be now?'

'I got some ideas,' replied Aaron, 'I even told one of them army officers, but he didn't seem too interested, 'specially after we didn't find it in the first cesspit.'

'Where?' asked Caleb.

'I reckon it's at the bottom of another pit,' said Aaron.

'What makes you think that?'

'Well, it just seemed kinda strange that Eli Carter's never wanted an old pit at the back of his place cleaned out since. He had a new one dug, claimin' that the old one was too near his house. Not only that, but when I told the army 'bout it, he showed them another one which I didn't know was there, but they never found nothin'. All I know is the one he showed the army sure warn't the one I knew about. I told 'em, but they wouldn't listen. Who the hell ever listens to a stupid nigger after he's been proven wrong twice?'

'Pencil and paper!' instructed Caleb. Pearl quickly produced the required items and Caleb told Aaron to draw a map of just where the pit was which he thought concealed the gold.

Aaron was not too adept with a pencil but, after a few attempts, he had drawn what he claimed was a passable plan of the area around the Carter homestead. He marked three crosses, one where the new cesspit was, one which Carter had shown to the army and the third which Aaron claimed was the disused pit likely to contain the gold. Caleb seemed satisfied and put the paper into his pocket.

'I'm goin' out there to take a look,' he announced. 'I'll likely as not be gone most of the day; in the meantime, you don't know where I've gone.'

'You is your own man,' grinned Pearl. 'It ain't for the likes of us to question what you do.'

'Ah hope you'll do us the honour of stayin' with us again,' said Aaron. 'There won't be no charge, we both insist on that, 'specially after you givin' us the fifty dollars.'

'Yes, Reverend,' smiled Pearl. 'That sure was generous of you. We ain't had chance to spend none of it yet, but we're plannin' a trip either in to Benson or Hawkesville. I'll buy the kids some new clothes, a pretty dress for me an' some decent gear for Aaron an' maybe treat ourselves to somethin' fancy what we don't really need at all.'

'You do that!' laughed Caleb. 'That's what money is for, spendin'. Sure, I'd be honoured to stay with you.'

'That's settled then!' beamed Pearl. 'Dinner'll be on the table about seven, spicy chicken, I knows you like that!'

'Nothin' could keep me away!' grinned Caleb.

'He's back!' George Baker announced in a very agitated voice as he crashed through the door of Eli Carter's house. 'He's back! Rode into town just like he owned the place. What the hell is he doin' back here an' where are those men you sent after him?'

'How the hell am I expected to know why

178

he's back and what happened?' demanded Carter, very annoyed that Baker had not seen fit to observe normal good manners.

'You assured me that he would be dealt with,' snarled Baker. 'Well, he sure don't look as though he's been dealt with, not unless he's a ghost.'

'George!' hissed Carter. 'Maybe I'd better remind you it was you who was all for just leavin' him alone. He'll just ride on, you said. Well you were wrong too. If he's back, Sven an' the boys shouldn't be too far behind, we'll wait to hear what they have to say.'

'I've got this feeling that you're never goin' to see Sven or the others again. I reckon they're dead and I reckon it was that damned preacher who killed them!'

Eli Carter remained thoughtful for a few moments and he finally came to the conclusion that Baker was probably correct. He knew he had told them that if they did not succeed in killing the preacher, they had no need to come back, but he knew that they would have done. They would have followed him back if only to try and kill him for no more than purely personal reasons.

'Mmmm...could be, I suppose,' Carter eventually agreed. 'OK, so we assume that he's killed them. Now we have to find out what he's come back to Reno for. It sure isn't for his health or because he likes the place. I'm goin' into town to ask a few questions. There's only two people likely to know what's goin' on, Matt McCauley and Aaron Williams.'

'Aaron Williams?' queried Baker.

'Sure, he's black ain't he? Matt may have been told what's goin' on, but I can't see him sayin' anythin', he's like that. A damned good sheriff, but too bloody honest. Williams is a different matter. If he knows anythin', it's gonna be easy to get him to talk.'

'How?' asked Baker.

Carter grinned. 'That shack of his, it'd flare up instantly if a lighted cheroot just happened to be dropped in the right place.'

'Preferably with him inside it!' grated Baker. 'He was the cause of that trouble in the first place; it sure was a good job we were a couple of days in front of the army. While we're in town, we'll check with Walter at the telegraph office. If anythin' is goin' on, he'll know for sure.'

'I reckon he would have told us by now if there had've been,' said Carter. 'Still, it's worth a check.'

Caleb peered over the crest of a small ridge about fifty yards from the house, just in time to see Baker riding furiously up to the door. He waited patiently until, to his surprise, both Baker and Eli Carter rode off towards Reno.

He allowed them enough time to get well clear and then waited a short while longer studying the house. There did not seem to be any sign of life, although he could not see if there was anyone else in the house or not. He decided that there was one way to find out.

There was a large black dog chained up at the back of the house and he reasoned that if there was anyone else about, its barking as he approached, would soon bring anyone out. In the event, the dog barked furiously and almost pulled the chain from its anchorage, but there was no movement from the house.

Consulting the rough map drawn by Aaron, he quickly located the first two cesspits, although they were both covered over by thick planks, but the third was not to be seen. Caleb widened the area of search, but there was still no sign of the pit and he was just beginning to come to the conclusion that perhaps Aaron had got it wrong when he noticed a pile of large, thick timbers alongside a barn. He stopped and looked at the pile thoughtfully and finally came to a decision.

Thick timbers, timber coverings across the other two cesspits; it was almost certain that the third pit would also be covered. Even so, there was no sign of covering. He looked again at the pile of timbers and thought.

He found a spade standing against a wall and proceeded to dig around the pile of timbers. At first it seemed that his idea was just that, an idea but, slamming the spade deep into the hard ground with one final thrust with all his strength behind it, the spade suddenly struck something very solid. A brief dig and examination showed splinters of timber.

There was no need to dig any further, he knew that he had discovered the third cesspit. Very carefully he replaced the earth and brushed it over to make it look as though it had never been disturbed. He said 'Greetings brother', to the dog as he passed, which simply set off another round of furious barking and chain pulling.

He rode back to Reno the way he had come and for a time he was puzzled at a plume of black smoke rising from the rubbish tip. He knew it was the rubbish tip even though he could not see it, that was all there was at that end of town. At first he assumed that Aaron must be burning something, but as he drew nearer, it was plain that it was far more serious than that. Urging his old horse into an unaccustomed gallop, he was soon racing across to the now almost burned-out shell of the Williams' shack.

Pearl and the children raced across to greet him, Pearl and her daughter weeping openly, but the boy was doing his best to keep his eyes dry, although he was fighting a losing battle.

'What happened?' shouted Caleb as he leapt off his horse.

'Eli Carter is what happened!' cried Pearl. 'Look at it! My home! I know it warn't much, but it was all we had and it was home! Why, what did we do?'

'You mean he deliberately set fire to it?' gasped Caleb.

'I knows he did!' Pearl cried again. 'I didn't see him do it, but I knows he did!'

'Where's Aaron?' demanded Caleb, looking wildly about. 'He isn't...?'

'No Reveren',' replied the boy, 'he went down into the town with Mr Baker.'

By that time almost the entire population of Reno had rushed up to see what was going on, although it was too late for anyone to do anything to save the shack. A couple of the women came over to comfort Pearl and her daughter, one of them even offering their barn to the family for a short while.

Sheriff McCauley appeared and walked around the smouldering wreckage a couple of times before asking Pearl what had happened. Pearl repeated her accusation against Eli Carter and in reply, he warned against making allegations she could not prove. He came across to the preacher.

'See what I mean about you causin' trouble!' grated McCauley.

'Are you accusing me of starting the fire?' smiled Caleb.

'You know damned well I'm not!' hissed McCauley. 'All I'm sayin' is this wouldn't 've happened if you hadn't showed up.'

'I fail to see just how my presence could be said to be responsible for this,' objected Caleb. 'I think Pearl is right, the man you should be talking to is Eli Carter. I agree with her, he started the fire deliberately.'

'Oh, so do I!' said McCauley. 'There's no doubt in my mind about that at all. Only trouble is, knowin' it an' provin' it are two totally different things. You know as well as I do that the shack was just waitin' for a spark.'

'And where is Carter now? For that matter, where is Aaron? Pearl said he went off with Baker.'

'Carter's in the saloon. I don't know where Aaron is, but if he was with Baker, the chances are they're all in the saloon.'

'Doesn't it strike you as odd that Aaron has not rushed up here to try and save what he could?'

'It's a free country,' shrugged McCauley.

'I suggest you do what you can to organize some accommodation for the family,' said Caleb. 'I'm off to the saloon!'

'I don't want no trouble!' warned the sheriff.

'Neither do I!' grinned Caleb. 'I can't speak for either Carter or Baker though!' He gave a derisive laugh and marched off down the street towards the saloon.

Matt McCauley had been right, Aaron Williams was in the saloon, sitting between Carter and Baker in a corner. Mick McCauley, the sheriff's twin brother, was lounging against the counter of the otherwise empty room, pretending that he was taking no notice of them but, in reality, his eagle eyes missed nothing. Aaron used the arrival of the preacher to remove himself from between the two men. There was hatred in his eyes, the first time Caleb had seen it in him. It was not directed at him, but at the two men who had kept him away from his family when they needed him.

'Ah suggests you is better off askin' the preacher yo'self!' he growled at them. 'Now, Ah'm goin' back to what's left of mah home an', Mr Eli Carter, if'n you knows what's good for you, you won't come nowheres near for a long time.'

Baker and Carter looked at each other and then at the preacher who was standing threateningly in the middle of the room, staring at them. It was clear they would have liked to have forced Aaron to stay but they knew they dare not stop him.

'Is Pearl OK, are my kids OK?' choked Aaron. Caleb nodded and patted Aaron on the shoulder.

'What's all this about?' he asked.

'They wanted me to tell 'em just what you was doin' back here!' glared Aaron. 'That shit Carter set fire to mah house; he tol' me he did, said it was nothin' to what was goin' to happen if'n Ah didn't tell them what I knew.'

'And did you?'

'You know me better'n that, Reveren'! 'Sides, I don't know nothin' do I?' He glowered at the two men. 'An' that's the truth, but you two is too stubborn to see it. Burnin' mah house down ain't got you nothin'!'

'Get back to Pearl,' said Caleb. 'I'll see you later; first, I think Mr Carter, Mr Baker and myself have some talking to do.'

'You just make sure that's all it is!' barked Mick McCauley. 'One sign of trouble from any one of you an' you're liable to get shot by me. You all got that?'

'There will be no trouble,' promised Caleb. 'I shan't start any and I doubt very much if either Carter or Baker have the guts to start any.' He marched over to the two other men and towered threateningly above them. 'If you wanted to know why I was back here, why didn't you ask me?' he barked. 'Aaron was telling the truth, he doesn't know a thing. As far as he's concerned all I am interested in is the gold you stole from the army. He thinks I'm looking for it for myself. I may be looking for it, but I can assure you I shall gain nothing from it, not even the reward.'

'What gold!' sneered Carter. 'The army had the same idea, but they never found nothin'.'

'Were you ever in the army?' Caleb asked, sitting opposite them and blocking off the means of escape.

'What's it to do with you?' demanded Carter.

'Nothing, I suppose,' agreed Caleb. 'I was just curious.'

'Sergeant Quartermaster, actually,' replied Carter.

'Interesting!' mused Caleb. 'If I were to guess, I'd say you were discharged for selling army property.'

'I was set up!' complained Carter. 'Anyhow, that's all over an' done with, I've been punished for that.'

'Mmmm...' mused Caleb again. 'Is that where you met Baker?' He looked at Baker and his smile caused Baker to worry even more than he was doing. 'Corporal Baker wasn't it? That's just about the nearest you ever came to being a colonel...'

'Colonel Baker!' insisted Baker. 'I have...'

'Documents to prove it!' agreed Caleb. 'The documents may well be genuine, but you are not. I know for a fact that you are or were, Corporal George Baker, although you were indeed in the Fifth Cavalry, you were, like your friend here, on the quartermaster's staff.'

'You're wastin' your time!' snarled Baker. 'There's no gold as far as the army is concerned and I have the papers to prove who I am!'

'No gold?' smiled Caleb. 'We shall see, we shall see!' He laughed loudly, stood up, raised his hat to them and said, 'Farewell, brothers!'

'What happened to my boys?' demanded

Carter as Caleb moved away.

'Oh, they're quite safe!' grinned Caleb. He did not enlighten them further.

It had been his intention to keep quiet about the gold and the fact that he knew Baker's true identity until the army arrived, but the burning of the Williams' shack had changed his mind. He wanted to see both men squirm, to force their hand. He was spoiling for a fight and, although he knew he should not, he would enjoy shooting them.

NINE

Aaron and his family were eventually rehoused in a disused house behind the church. It had belonged to the last preacher to have lived in Reno. Work needed to be done on the structure, but there were more than enough promises to help, although Caleb had discovered that when it actually came to calling on that help, other matters suddenly assumed greater urgency. Nevertheless, Pearl seemed quite happy with the house and Aaron was sure he would be able to effect any repairs on his own. Pearl's greatest sadness was the loss of all her personal bits and pieces.

Both Eli Carter and George Baker were very noticeable by their absence for the remainder of the day. They had last been seen riding out to Carter's ranch after making dark threats of retribution upon that 'nigger preacher!'

Even with the statement from Aaron Williams that Carter had admitted to starting the fire deliberately, Matt McCauley refused to act, saying that he needed something far more substantial than the word of someone like Aaron, hastening to add that he could not take the word of anyone alone, no matter what their colour was.

That evening, quite miraculously Caleb considered, Pearl Williams somehow managed to provide an excellent meal of spicy chicken and rice and, over the meal, he was quite relieved to hear that they had lost no money in the fire and that the few valuable things they had lost were probably what few clothes they had.

The new house had some furniture already in it, mainly tables, chairs and cupboards. There were no beds, but Aaron managed to find some decent timbers and had soon constructed four makeshift bunks. Actually, Pearl quite liked the idea of living in the house, it was larger than their shack had been and it had the luxury of three bedrooms upstairs and its own water pump just outside the kitchen door. Previously, they had had to carry water from a well some distance away from the shack.

Later, when he went to the saloon to purchase another bottle of whisky—the other one had been a casualty of the flames—Caleb discovered from Matt Mc-Cauley, that nobody knew who owned either church or house, so Aaron was welcome to stay at least until someone could prove title, which was most unlikely. Armed with this good news, the whisky, a bottle of wine which claimed to be of French origin for Pearl and a box of cheroots, they celebrated the night in style, even claiming the fire to be a blessing.

'How much do you reckon he really knows?' asked a very worried George Baker as he and Eli Carter also attacked a bottle of whisky and some large cigars.

'Well he sure knows just who the hell you are!' hissed Carter. 'The more important question is just who the hell else knows.'

'Bastard!' spat Baker. 'Of all the men

to pass through, why did he have to know just who the real Colonel Baker was?'

'You should've kept a low profile,' said Carter. 'I was always warnin' you about that but no, you always had to show off, play the big man, let everyone know you were supposed to be a colonel. I said someone might just know, but you wouldn't hear of it. Now look what a mess your struttin' has got us into.'

'Got you into? It seems to me that it's me who's likely to end up in trouble; you ain't never claimed to be somebody you're not and been drawin' a pension you're not entitled to.'

'No, but I'm sure as hell implicated in that gold.'

George Baker laughed. 'Bullshit! That's all that preacher is doin', he's bullshittin'. They've looked once for it and never found it and you know the army as well as I do, they won't act unless they've got somethin' to go on. Nobody knows where the gold is and, providin' we sit tight for another couple of years, nobody is gonna be any the wiser.'

'Yeh? Maybe so,' muttered Carter, 'but I have this sickenin' feelin' that everythin's about to fall round our ears.'

'Then you should've sent men out who could do the job!' sneered Baker. 'I still reckon that if you hadn't sent them out after him, he'd've ridden on an' forgotten all about us. Tryin' to kill a man like that is useless, he's bound to come back an' find out why.'

'Then maybe you'd better do the job yourself!' muttered Carter.

'Maybe I'll do just that!' grated Baker.

Caleb had the distinct feeling that he was being watched, but there was no sign of anyone. He was surveying the wreckage of the shack along with Pearl and her daughter. They were looking more in hope than expectation for any small items that may have escaped the flames or at least not be too badly damaged. In fact, Pearl was overjoyed to find that a trunk which had been under their bed, was almost untouched. It contained most of her and her children's clothing.

The feeling of being watched persisted, although he did not tell Pearl as he did not want to cause any alarm. He excused himself from the search and moved slowly and casually towards a small ridge some fifty or so yards away but, when he was within about twenty yards, he suddenly found himself crashing to the ground as something thudded into his shoulder. He had the impression that he had heard a shot at almost the same time as he had felt the impact, but he could not be certain and it was not important, the important thing was that he had been shot.

He did not know if the shot had been heard down in the town or not, it was quite possible that it had not. He saw a face appear briefly above the ridge and he decided that the safest thing to do was to pretend he was dead. It seemed to work, since the face disappeared. It might have been very brief, but he had recognized George Baker.

Pearl was at his side, crying out hysterically and it was all that he could do to make her stop, assuring her that apart from the pain in his shoulder, he was otherwise unhurt. It seemed that someone in Reno had heard the shot, as shortly afterwards Matt McCauley was gazing down at him.

'Looks like they missed!' grinned McCauley.

'It sure doesn't feel like they did,' muttered Caleb, still on the ground. 'Anyhow, you sound as though you're disappointed.'

'It could just be that I am!' grinned McCauley. 'Come on, I guess we'd better have Doc Sharp take a look at you.'

'I suppose that means he's got to do some digging,' moaned Caleb. 'I know the bullet's still in there.'

Matt McCauley laughed. 'Hell, Mr Preacher, I do believe you're scared! I didn't think there was anythin' you was scared of, but I reckon the thought of havin' a bullet dug out scares you stiff!'

'I have no fear of death,' muttered Caleb, struggling to his feet, 'and I have no fear of any man, any man that is except a doctor armed with a scapel.'

'You're not alone in that,' laughed the sheriff, 'but I really did think there was nothin' that could scare you.'

'At least you know I'm human,' grunted Caleb. 'See...' He placed his hand on his shoulder and showed it, wet with blood, to the sheriff. 'I've even got blood in my veins just like any other man and, despite what anyone may say, my blood is exactly the same as the blood of a white man.'

'Yeh!' laughed McCauley. 'Your shit stinks just the same as well. OK, you don't have to convince me. I don't suppose you saw who shot you?'

'George Baker!' said Caleb, firmly. 'I saw him all right.'

'Then I guess I'll just have to fetch him in.'

'That's up to you, Sheriff,' sighed Caleb. 'I don't think it will get you very far though, it will be my word against his, unless anyone else saw him.' He turned to Pearl and her daughter. 'I don't suppose either of you saw anythin'?'

'All we heard was the shot,' said Pearl, 'an' all we saw was you fallin'.'

'You saw him though,' said McCauley. 'Men have been arrested on less evidence than that.'

'Is my word better than Pearl's then?'

'Don't know what you mean?'

'She saw Carter set fire to her place, but that wasn't good enough for you, so why should I be any different?'

'Well...'cos...' faltered the sheriff. ''Cos you're a preacher!'

'That makes a difference does it?' sneered Caleb. 'Don't bother, Sheriff, even if you do arrest Baker, I shall deny seeing him, it just isn't worth the bother.'

'It's your problem!' muttered McCauley, smarting a little from the obvious rebuke. 'Come on, you're still losin' blood, Doc Sharp had better look at it quick.'

Despite the fear of doctors, Caleb had no alternative but to submit to the tender mercies of Doc Sharp. Actually, he found that the doc was really quite gentle and the operation to remove the bullet, which was buried quite deep, was nowhere near as painful as he had expected. He had been offered a bottle of whisky to drink before the operation, but Caleb refused this crude means of deadening the pain. It was more his pride would not let him drink the whisky; he wanted to show everyone that he could take the pain. Pride was probably Caleb's biggest failing.

He was allowed to rest for a while before being sent out, during which time Pearl and Aaron maintained a constant vigil at his side. It was only when a protesting voice in the street outside was heard that all of them, including Caleb, went to the window.

'Looks like the sheriff has arrested Colonel Baker,' said Pearl.

'I told him it would be a waste of time,' grunted Caleb. 'Come on, I feel fine now...'

He did not, but he was not prepared to admit it. 'Let's see what it's all about.'

Sheriff McCauley had indeed arrested George Baker, but not for the shooting of the preacher. When Caleb arrived at the sheriff's office, McCauley triumphantly produced a bar of gold.

'I found it in his desk!' he beamed. 'I reckon it's part of the gold the army was looking for.'

Baker had been locked in a cell and was vehemently claiming that the gold was nothing to do with the army.

Caleb picked up the bar and studied it. He produced the piece of paper he had written the numbers on in Colonel Oliver's office, checked again and shook his head.

'I don't know where this gold came from,' he said, 'but the markings don't tie up with the army gold.'

'There, I told you so!' screamed Baker. 'I told you, I bought that years ago as an investment.'

'Where'd you get those numbers and markin's from?' demanded the sheriff. 'As far as I know, the army never released them.'

'They didn't!' grinned Caleb. 'I was just lucky, they were on the file in Colonel Oliver's office, I copied them when he wasn't there.'

McCauley grunted. 'For a preacher, you sure are mighty devious. I still don't know for sure, so I'm holdin' Baker until I can check it out officially.'

'It looks like you'll be able to do that straightaway,' said Caleb, cocking his head to one side. 'By the sound of things, I'd say the army has just arrived.'

Caleb was right. The whole town suddenly seemed alive with the blue coats of soldiers. What appeared to be at least a hundred of them, when the dust had settled and they had dismounted, turned out to be twenty. A dust-covered officer brushed himself down, saw the preacher as he came out of the sheriff's office and came over to them.

'Colonel Benjamin Oliver,' he proclaimed, saluting the sheriff. 'You must be Sheriff McCauley; you, Preacher, I know.'

'We were expectin' you,' said McCauley. 'I reckon you and your men could do with a drink after your ride. They can go over to my brother's place, the saloon. They can have a beer on the house, I'll square it with Mick.'

'Mighty civil of you, Sheriff,' beamed the

colonel. 'Lieutenant!' he called. 'There's drinks for the men in the saloon, you'd better join me and the sheriff.'

'Yes sir!' responded the lieutenant and he ordered the men into the saloon. They did not need any second bidding.

McCauley led the way back into his office where he produced a bottle of whisky and poured out four glasses full. After dusting themselves off again, the officers sat down opposite the desk. Caleb chose to stand against the wall.

'I suppose the Reverend here has told you why we've come?' Colonel Oliver said to McCauley, who nodded. 'This so-called Colonel George Baker you have living here, it is my belief that he is not who he claims to be. We think he is, in fact, an ex-corporal also called George Baker.'

'You can ask him yourself,' grinned the sheriff, nodding behind him. 'That's him behind them bars!'

Both the colonel and the lieutenant looked very surprised and stared at the now subdued figure of George Baker.

'What is he doing in your cell?' asked the lieutenant.

The sheriff produced the bar of gold, sliding it across the desk to the colonel. 'I reckon this is part of the gold you've been lookin' for,' he said. 'I found it in his desk.'

The colonel examined the gold and smiled. 'Very nice, but it's not one of ours. I'm surprised you didn't know that.'

'How should I know somethin' like that?' asked McCauley. 'You never gave out the markin's.'

The colonel laughed and looked at the preacher. 'I would have thought the Reverend Black would have been able to tell you.'

'Me, Colonel!' exclaimed Caleb. 'How should I know more than anyone else?' He gave the colonel a broad grin.

Colonel Oliver coughed slightly, gave a quick glance at his lieutenant and addressed the gold bar again. 'Quite!' he muttered. 'However, this is not our gold, I can assure you of that.'

'What did I tell you!' shouted Baker.

'Now let me out of here, McCauley, you've got nothing to hold me on now.'

'On the contrary,' said Colonel Oliver. 'You claim to be Colonel George Baker, late of the Fifth Cavalry. In fact we do know you to be Corporal George Baker, also late of the Fifth Cavalry.'

'You can't prove nothin'!' roared Baker. 'I've got papers to prove who I am...'

'Lieutenant!' interrupted Colonel Oliver. 'Have you ever seen this man before?'

'No, sir,' replied the lieutenant.

'I'm not surprised!' snarled Baker. 'I've never seen him either! Anyway, he's too young, he couldn't've been in the army when I was.'

'I quite agree,' smiled Oliver. 'But one thing I do find very surprising is that you should not recognize your own son, if you are indeed Colonel George Baker.'

'Son!' exclaimed Baker. He stared hard at the lieutenant for a moment before sinking slowly on to the bench at the back of the cell. 'You mean...' he choked.

'Precisely,' said Colonel Oliver. 'This is the son of the real George Baker.'

207

Baker looked dumbly at the floor for a few moments. Eventually he looked up and glared hatred at the preacher. 'None of this would ever have happened if you hadn't decided to pass through Reno!' he spat. 'May your soul rot in hell.'

'It may well do,' smiled Caleb. 'So you admit you are not the real Colonel George Baker?'

'Don't look like I got much choice!' grumbled Baker. 'Yeh, you're right, I am Corporal George Baker. I took the place of the real colonel after I'd killed him.'

'Killed him?' queried Colonel Oliver.

'He found out how we'd taken the gold,' said Baker. 'By that time we had both left the army though.'

'I think we can add a charge of murder,' smiled the colonel. 'Now, where is the gold?'

Baker laughed loudly. 'That's the rub, Colonel, I don't know!'

'Don't know?' demanded the sheriff and Caleb together.

'That's right, I don't know!' repeated Baker, laughing again. 'Carter's the only one who does know, he moved it after Williams found it. I don't know where he put it, he'd never tell me.'

'And this?' asked McCauley, indicating the bar of gold on his desk.

'Just like I told you,' said Baker. 'I bought that as an investment, it's genuine enough, it belongs to me.'

'I don't suppose you'll have much use for it where you're goin',' said McCauley. 'I'll have it taken to the bank. Don't worry, it'll be in your name.'

'Well that was sorted out a lot easier than I expected,' said Colonel Oliver. 'I suggest we go and see this Mr Carter.'

Once outside, Caleb just had to ask the colonel how he had managed to come up with Colonel Baker's son so quickly. 'I must admit to being rather surprised,' said Caleb. 'I seem to remember the colonel saying that he had no children.'

'He hadn't!' grinned Colonel Oliver.

'Then who...'

'Lieutenant Eric Baker,' introduced the colonel. 'Baker is a common enough name, it wasn't hard to find him. He's no relation at all to Colonel Baker.'

'But you told...' croaked the sheriff.

'Did I, Sheriff?' winked the colonel. 'All I heard was your George Baker admitting he was impersonating the late Colonel George Baker.'

'Come to think of it,' sighed McCauley, 'that's all I heard too. How about you, Reverend?'

Caleb stuck his finger in his ear and waggled it furiously. 'It's strange, but I suffer from wax. It makes hearing things very difficult.'

TEN

'OK,' said Colonel Oliver, 'we've got Baker on a charge of drawing an army pension to which he was not entitled and we could possibly lay a charge of murder against him, but that was not the prime reason I was allowed to come here. I managed to convince my superiors that I had a good chance of recovering that gold. You said you had a good idea where it was, Reverend, I hope you still have. Where is it?'

'Where it has been almost all the time,' replied Caleb, just hoping that he was not wrong. 'In a cesspit on Carter's ranch.'

'We checked them before,' sighed the sheriff. 'What makes you think it's still there?'

'You checked two pits,' said Caleb, 'but I know where there's a third.'

'That's what Aaron Williams reckoned,'

grunted McCauley. 'We looked but we never found one.'

'But this time I think I know exactly where it is,' grinned Caleb. 'I suppose I could be wrong, but I don't think so.'

'Well there's one way of finding out for sure,' said Colonel Oliver. 'We go and dig it out.'

'I hope your men don't mind gettin' covered in shit!' grinned Caleb. 'I'll show you where it is, but don't expect me to help empty it.'

'That's what they joined the army to do,' laughed the colonel, 'get everybody else out of the shit. Lieutenant, go tell the men to mount up, we're going prospecting for gold.'

It seemed that Eli Carter was expecting them and he seemed quite confident, even offering to show them the sites of the cesspits. However, his confidence changed to alarm when Caleb turned down the offer and directed the lieutenant to the side of the barn.

Eli Carter had tried to hide his alarm,

but Caleb had not missed it and he stood beside Carter as the soldiers began their digging and he suggested to Carter that it would be just as well to admit things there and then. Carter simply scowled but said nothing.

The heavy beams were quickly uncovered and Carter's manner became increasingly agitated until, eventually, he stormed off into the house. Something told Caleb to follow him and keep an eye on him. He automatically loosened one of his guns in its holster, fortunately the one hand he was best with, and followed Carter into what he assumed was his study or office.

'Baker should've killed you!' snarled Carter, pouring himself a large glass of whisky. He did not offer one to the preacher. 'He wasn't sure if he had or not. Pity, with you out of the way nobody would've known where to look.' He took a long drink, coughed and choked and, wiping his mouth on his sleeve, he stared hard at Caleb. 'Anyhow, just how the hell did you know about that pit?'

'Aaron Williams maintained there was

another,' smiled Caleb, 'and I can think of no reason why he should lie about something like that. I was out here yesterday, when you rode off and set fire to his place. It wasn't hard to find; I can't think why nobody found it before.'

'Because they were nothin' but dumb soldiers!' sneered Carter. 'They aren't expected to think for themselves, they even have to fart by numbers!'

'Well it looks like some dumb soldiers are about to uncover the gold you thought was safe,' laughed Caleb.

'Only 'cos you poked your nose in where it wasn't wanted!'

Caleb laughed again. 'The Lord works in mysterious ways, He truly does. If those three outlaws hadn't tried to rob my congregation, the chances are none of this would ever have happened.'

'An' if that idiot, George Baker, hadn't pretended he was somebody he wasn't!' snarled Carter. 'I did warn him, but no he had to play-act. He was obsessed with the idea of being a colonel; why the hell that should be I don't know, but he was.'

'Well, he's under arrest,' said Caleb, 'and I suspect it will only be a short time now before you are.'

Carter snorted contemptuously pouring himself another large whisky. This time he sneeringly offered the preacher the bottle, but it was refused. Carter flopped into a chair and stared out of the window, ignoring Caleb.

The task of emptying the cesspit took almost two hours and when they did finally reach the solid ground underneath, there was a sudden cry from one of the men as he picked out a very tarnished piece of metal. It was taken from him by the lieutenant and dropped into a bucket of cold water to wash off the offending excrement and then given to Colonel Oliver. The numbers and markings on the bar were checked against the list the colonel had and he gave a grunt of satisfaction and immediately ordered the men to continue looking. Ten minutes later thirty gold bars were standing in a pile, all carefully washed and checked.

Caleb had come out of the house at the first shout and Colonel Oliver, a broad smile on his face, warmly shook the preacher by the hand and then proceeded to give orders about the shipment of the gold back to Fort Benson. They had brought a wagon with them and it was loaded on to that, along with six heavily armed soldiers. The soldiers who had been emptying the pit were allowed to strip off and wash themselves down, although the stench was still very strong on their clothing. Colonel Oliver promised them new clothes when they returned.

'Where's Eli Carter?' asked a very happy Colonel Oliver. 'He's got a lot of questions to answer, he's goin' back with us.'

'He should be in the house,' replied Caleb. 'I'll go fetch him. It could be that he'll need to be carried, he was drinking heavily when I left him.'

It was apparent that Eli Carter was completely incapable. He had finished the one bottle of whisky and had started on another and Caleb had to carry him out of the house. He dumped the almost lifeless body on to the wagon, along with the gold.

However, Colonel Oliver was taking no chances and ordered that Carter be securely bound. There were a few formalities to complete at the sheriff's office in Reno, but by mid-afternoon, the troop was ready to leave. Colonel Oliver had considered allowing the men to remain in Reno for the night, but security of the gold was far more important, so he ordered them to ride until sunset.

With little reason to remain in Reno, Caleb too decided to ride with the soldiers back to Benson. He had to go there anyway to collect the reward.

During the journey, Eli Carter recovered and threatened the preacher with empty threats of death, maintaining that he would hunt the preacher down for the remainder of his life. Caleb laughed and suggested that even if he did complete his term in prison, the chances were that his, Carter's, life could well be very short. George Baker remained almost completely silent throughout the whole journey back to Benson.

News that the gold bars had been recovered seemed to reach Benson even before the soldiers did, which did not surprise Caleb at all, although it seemed something of a mystery to Colonel Oliver.

Caleb could imagine the sudden increase in activity on the telegraph wires. The telegraphist in Reno, if not Sheriff Mc-Cauley, would have passed the message on which, in turn, would have been relayed to other towns almost immediately. He was quite certain that they even knew about it in the State capital by now.

There were crowds of curious onlookers lining the streets as the troop approached the fort, although quite what they expected to see was something of a mystery. There was great speculation as to how the gold had been found, the most popular story being that the soldiers had been engaged in a raging gun battle with at least thirty outlaws. The fact that there were only two men under obvious arrest seemed to disappoint the crowds.

However, the crowds did have one fact right, although where the information had come from so quickly did seem a mystery, they all knew that it was a black preacher who had led the soldiers to the gold and that he, the preacher, was going to get the $50,000 reward.

The result was, that after leaving the fort having completed all the necessary formalities, Caleb was besieged by people pressing him for money for this good cause and that good cause. Suddenly Caleb Black, Preacher, was the toast of the town. Even the whores pressed their business, although with no effect. Shop keepers were more than ready to offer him all the credit he wanted and the three other ministers of religion seemed to be rivalling each other to invite him to speak in their churches, all pointing out that funds were urgently required for this project or that.

Alone and aloof from all this sudden adulation, Sister Claire at the orphanage seemed to be the only person in Benson who made no approach to Caleb.

Caleb had already decided what he was going to do with the reward money and, much as he would have liked to, he was not intending to keep it for himself. He had long dreamed of having enough money to be able to settle somewhere and live a life of comparative ease, but he was resigned to the fact that on this occasion, his dream was not going to be fulfilled.

There were only two problems to his good intentions, the first that it was just possible that there was some technical reason why he should not receive the reward and the other that the army would be so desperate to get their hands on the orphanage building that they would be prepared to pay even more. He deliberately avoided any contact with Sister Claire or any of the nuns until he could be sure of what was happening.

It was two days before he received a summons from the fort that Colonel Oliver wanted to see him and, although not normally a nervous man, he could not control his feelings of apprehension and anticipation as he was shown to the colonel's office.

'I want you to meet General Graham,'

said Colonel Oliver as the preacher was shown into his office. 'He wanted to meet you and thank you personally for what you have done.'

General Graham was a surprisingly short man, although quite stout and, after shaking hands with him, Caleb quickly sat down so as not to be seeming to intimidate the man by his own enormous stature. After showing some surprise at the preacher's size, the general seemed somewhat relieved when they were all seated. Colonel Oliver produced a bottle which bore the legend 'Champagne' and poured out three glasses of the pale, bubbly contents. A toast to Caleb was proposed by the general and, after a few minor pleasantries, the discussion became more serious.

'Fifty thousand is a lot of money,' said General Graham. 'What do you intend doing with it? Perhaps you would like to set up your own church somewhere, or even simply retire?'

'I think I can account for almost every cent of it,' said Caleb. 'By my reckoning

I should only have about five thousand for myself and I don't suppose that will last too long.'

'Five thousand?' queried the general. 'What on earth are you going to do with the other forty-five thousand?'

'Hopefully, buy some property I have my eye on,' grinned Caleb, nodding slightly at Colonel Oliver. 'That's going to take care of forty thousand, the other five thousand rightly belongs to a man back in Reno. Without his knowledge I don't think the gold would have ever been found.'

'The man, Williams?' asked Colonel Oliver.

'That's right,' nodded Caleb. 'I think five thousand will set him up for the remainder of his life, any more and he'd just be lost. He wants to set himself up as a blacksmith, I reckon this should see that he does.'

'Very noble of you,' smiled the general. 'Forty thousand on buying property seems an awful lot. Just where is this property?'

'Right here in Benson,' grinned Caleb. 'It may seem a lot, but I hear the army is prepared to pay about thirty-five thousand for some property as well.'

'Yes...well...' faltered the general, 'that may have been the case a few days ago, but things have a habit of changing even overnight.'

Caleb scented victory. 'Does that mean you're not interested in buying the orphanage?' he asked.

'Oh, we'd still like the building,' admitted General Graham, 'but it seems that Washington has had second thoughts.'

'Perhaps I had better explain to the preacher, General?' offered Colonel Oliver. General Graham nodded, he was plainly ill at ease in being questioned by a civilian, especially on matters concerning the army. 'It seems that Washington have objected to the proposed price of the property,' continued Colonel Oliver. 'They have ordered that no more than twenty-five thousand be spent on the purchase. They point out, rightly, that we would have a duty to the orphans, we could not simply cast them on to the streets—not that we had intended doing so!' he added, hastily.

'They point out that the measure is purely temporary in any event.'

Caleb grinned broadly. 'Temporary, how temporary is temporary?'

'You have been a soldier,' said the colonel, 'would you be willing to put a time on such a thing?' Caleb smiled and shook his head. 'Then neither can we, not even General Graham.'

'And what would you do if you could not buy the property?'

'Build new barracks and accommodation where we're goin' to anyway,' grunted General Graham. 'Colonel Oliver has acquainted me with your interest in the orphanage. Make your bid, Mr Black, I for one will lose no sleep over the army's loss, I was against the plan anyway, I consider it most unsuitable and not at all secure.'

'Before I can do that, I have to have the money,' reminded Caleb. 'So far you have talked about what I intend doing with it, but I have not seen the colour of it yet.'

General Graham laughed self-consciously, took a piece of paper from his coat and handed it to Caleb. 'Obviously we cannot give you cash here,' he explained, 'but that is as good as cash. It is a banker's draft. All you have to do is take it to the bank, almost any bank, it will be honoured.'

Caleb had handled banker's drafts before and knew their worth. 'I thank you, General, I shall go straight round to the bank and start arranging things. I thank you too, Colonel,' he said, smiling at Colonel Oliver. 'Without your faith in me, we would not be sitting here now and you wouldn't have recovered the gold.'

'Ah, yes,' said Colonel Oliver, 'that leads us to another matter. Both Baker and Carter are to stand trial. We're not sure if it will be a military trial or a civil trial at this precise moment, but I think it likely to be a military trial, especially since Baker was a serving soldier when the gold disappeared. Obviously you are a vital witness and we shall be requiring your presence to give evidence.'

'How long?' asked Caleb. He was not surprised and it was true that he was probably the chief witness.

'Before the trial starts? No more than

a week I should think,' said General Graham. 'I can't see it lasting too long either, maybe two or three days.'

'That means I just about have time to go to Reno and give Aaron his money,' said Caleb and, on noting the alarmed look on the face of General Graham, he added, 'Don't worry, General, I'll be back. It certainly is not in my interest to see either Baker or Carter out free. Besides, knowing how long legal matters like buying property take, I reckon I'll be here at least a month.'

'I'd prefer it if you deferred going back to Reno until after the trial,' said the general. 'Not that I mistrust you in any way, but it is quite possible that there will be questions and statements to be taken before the trial.'

'Not that you mistrust me!' grinned Caleb. 'I'll buy that, you don't really trust me...'

He raised a hand to stifle the general's objection. 'Don't worry, it doesn't bother me, I can't say that I have implicit trust in my fellow man either and I have even less trust in the army. You're right, I'd better be here just in case the army suddenly decide to increase their bid.'

'Then on that note of mutual distrust,' laughed Colonel Oliver, 'I must ask you to leave us, Mr Black. I think you will find that the bank is expecting you. The corporal will escort you out. Once again, on behalf of the army, General Graham and myself, I thank you for all you have done.'

'I hope they make you a general for your part in getting the gold back,' smiled Caleb. Colonel Oliver was obviously embarrassed and muttered something neither Caleb nor General Graham could understand.

Caleb stood up and gazed down at the diminutive figure of General Graham and he could not resist the urge to simply tower over the man. He did so while he made a show of donning his hat. He then laughed loudly and left the office.

The bank had been prepared for the preacher and he was fawned on and offered tea, a beverage the manager obviously thought fitting for a man of the cloth. Caleb expressed the wish that it was something stronger, which seemed to cause the manager considerable alarm, but a whisky bottle was somehow discovered in a drawer.

'Now,' fussed the manager, 'you are a rich man now. If you are not used to handling money, it can be all too easy to lose it by stupid deals or even simply spending it...'

'I know exactly what I intend doin' with it!' sighed Caleb. 'If anyone else asks me what I'm going to do with it, I swear I'll end up killing them. Why is it you suddenly find you've got lots of friends and willing advisers when you've got money? If it wasn't for that reward, there's hardly a soul in Benson who would give me a second look.' He leaned forward and glared at the manager, making him cringe in his chair. 'I'll tell you exactly what I want you to do. Now listen very carefully...'

Caleb made himself very clear about what he wanted and, despite his obvious disapproval, the manager of the bank nodded weakly and accepted it all. It appeared that the bank was also handling the sale of the orphanage and the manager's attitude suddenly changed as he saw two lots of commission coming his way. He tried insisting that the army's offer of $35,000 still stood, but he eventually discovered a piece of paper which he had 'Forgotten about' and agreed that they had reduced their offer to $25,000. A price of $30,000 was eventually settled on. That left an extra $10,000 which Caleb was tempted to keep for himself, but he eventually decided that Sister Claire could put $10,000 to far better use than he could.

Out in the street, he was suddenly confronted by Sheriff Jordan, who had clearly been waiting for him. 'You've got trouble!' said Jordan. 'Sven Olfsen and Adam Smith have broken out of jail!'

'How?' demanded Caleb.

'Somehow they managed to unlock their cell,' muttered Jordan. 'They either picked the lock or they somehow got hold of a duplicate key, I can't say for sure.'

'The other two?'

'Still locked up,' assured Jordan. 'They're secure enough, I've even put padlocks on their cell. The thing is, they knocked out my deputy, Sinclair, an' stole guns and ammunition. Sinclair reckons he heard them say somethin' about killin' you.'

'When was this?' muttered Caleb, instinctively feeling his injured shoulder and realizing that he would probably be unable to use his left hand.

'Two hours ago!' said the sheriff. 'I was in court when it happened.'

'Any idea where they are now?'

'None at all. Look, you'd better come to my office 'til we catch them.'

'No thanks!' said Caleb. 'Thanks for the warning though.'

'You'll be safer there!' urged Jordan, more concerned that he should not have a murder on his hands than for any real concern about the safety of the preacher.

'I thank you for your concern!' laughed Caleb. 'However, I would prefer to take my chance out on the street.'

'Please yourself!' grunted Jordan. 'I've warned you, that's the main thing. I can't force you.'

Caleb laughed as a thought struck him. 'How much are they worth this time?'

'That's somethin' we ain't had the time to even think about,' grunted the sheriff. 'I'd say at least the same though.'

'Three hundred dollars!' grinned Caleb. 'It hardly seems worth bothering, especially just after having been given fifty thousand. Is that dead or alive?'

'Whichever way you choose to bring 'em in!' grinned the sheriff. 'Sure you can manage this time? I see you're nursin' an injured shoulder.'

'I can manage!' assured Caleb. 'Don't let that stop you from bringing them in if you can though. I certainly won't complain at the loss of three hundred dollars.'

'Then maybe I'd better get them before you do, for their sakes!' grinned Jordan.

Duly warned, Caleb decided that it was time he found the courage to face Sister Claire and he went along to the orphanage. He was a little surprised when it was Sister

Claire herself who opened the door for him, but the warning flash in her eyes told him exactly where Sven Olfsen and Adam Smith were. Taking the hint, he touched the brim of his hat and apologized, saying that he had just remembered that he had to be back at the bank and that he would see her later.

He was a few yards up the street when he heard them behind him. The expected thud of a bullet in his back did not materialize and he slowly turned and, on looking up at the first-floor window, he laughed loudly at the men.

'When will you ever learn?' he called. 'Outwitted by a bunch of nuns again!'

The two men glowered up at the window and the rifle that was aimed at them from it. 'Still hidin' behind women's skirts!' jeered Smith. 'I think the time has come to test just whether that nun up there is capable of squeezin' that trigger. Reckon you can, Sister?' he called up to her.

Caleb was ready; both men moved suddenly and swiftly, but not as swift as the preacher. Had he been able to use both his guns, Caleb had little doubt that he could have easily taken both men. As it was, he saw Adam Smith crash to the ground just before everything went blank about him...

'He's coming to, Sister!'

A voice echoed those welcome words somewhere in the inner recesses of Caleb's brain. For a few moments he stared at the hazy shape hovering above him and slowly managed to bring it into focus.

He would not have been too surprised to have discovered that he was dead and was looking at an angel but, as the face became clearer, he recognized it as belonging to Sister Claire. He grinned weakly and winced with pain. This time the pain came from his other shoulder, which forced him to laugh dryly.

'I guess I can't use either hand now! What happened?'

'You happened!' scolded Sister Claire. 'You killed one of them, the one called Smith. Hardly fitting for a man of God!'

'I think He'll understand!' grinned Caleb. 'Olfsen?'

'Back in jail where he belongs!' fussed the sister. 'Sister Benedict is a very good shot, she managed to shoot the gun out of his hand, after he'd shot you of course. He'll be quite disappointed he didn't kill you.'

'I imagine he will be!' laughed Caleb, once again wincing with pain. 'How long have I been here and where, exactly, am I?'

'You are in a room in the orphanage,' said Sister Claire. 'You have been unconscious for about an hour, that's all.'

'Nice room,' grinned Caleb, looking about and once again wincing at the effort. 'You can keep this one specially for me.'

'Why especially for you?'

'Well, I do own the place now! Well, as good as.'

'You?' exclaimed Sister Claire.

'Why not?' grinned Caleb. 'I'm sure you heard that I'd come into a lot of money all of a sudden. If you didn't hear, you must have been the only ones in the State who didn't.'

'We heard!' smiled Sister Claire. 'So, you've bought the orphanage, what are you going to do with it?'

'Me, Sister?' Caleb laughed and choked. 'Me, I'm going to do absolutely nothing. I don't know the first thing about orphanages or orphans. It's you who's going to do something with it. The place is yours for as long as you need it. I'll even throw in another ten thousand dollars!'

'Mr Black!' said Sister Claire, sternly. 'We are not used to practical jokes...'

'Who's joking, Sister!'

As far as she could remember, Sister Claire had never kissed a man before, not even her father. The experience, new as it was, made her blush brightly and run out of the room to hide her embarrassment. It was impossible to tell if Caleb was blushing or not, but he too had to admit that he could well have been.

This Large Print Book for the Partially sighted, who cannot read normal print, is published under the auspices of

THE ULVERSCROFT FOUNDATION

THE ULVERSCROFT FOUNDATION

. . . we hope that you have enjoyed this Large Print Book. Please think for a moment about those people who have worse eyesight problems than you . . . and are unable to even read or enjoy Large Print, without great difficulty.

You can help them by sending a donation, large or small to:

**The Ulverscroft Foundation,
1, The Green, Bradgate Road,
Anstey, Leicestershire, LE7 7FU,
England.**

or request a copy of our brochure for more details.

The Foundation will use all your help to assist those people who are handicapped by various sight problems and need special attention.

Thank you very much for your help.